CW01456811

# Between Silences

## ELOUISE BAXTER

To Marilyn,

With Love

Louise
xxx

Copyright © 2024 by Elouise Baxter

All rights reserved.

No part of this publication may be reproduced, distributed, or transmitted in any form or by any means, including photocopying, other electronic or mechanical methods, without the prior written permission of the author

This is a work of fiction. The story, all names, characters, and events portrayed in this production are fictitious. No identification with actual persons (living or deceased) is purely coincidental.

*For those of you who sometimes feel lost in your own mind, never stop trying to find yourself.*

# Content Warnings

This book contains conversations of grief, descriptions of gore and mentions of murder.

For anyone who may be sensitive to these topics, please continue with caution. You are not alone. Visit https://www.mind. org.uk/

# Chapter One

## ELLIE

*appy Birthday to you... Happy Birthday to you... Happy Birthday dear Ellie...Happy Birthday to you!*
They surrounded my desk with an obnoxiously pink cake with a pair of handcuffs drawn onto it in thick, sweet icing. The same cake that every single other person in the team gets whenever it's their birthday. I awkwardly sat waiting for their singing to cease with a grin plastered onto my face as forcibly as I possibly could.

"Thank you. Thank you." I flung my hand in the 'stop, stop' motion, forcing a laugh out of me too.

"We got you a team present as a way to say a simple thank you for everything you do for the team." Carly, my desk neighbour and best friend piped up, handing me a messily wrapped gift stuffed into a gift bag. I hastily unwrapped it, trying to look as excited as I possibly could before pulling out a box and revealed a 'World's best co-worker' mug. The perfect gift, another mug to add to my never-ending stack of co-worker mugs.

"It's great, thank you." I nodded, pushing it into the corner of my desk.

A loud cough echoed from the other side of the office, a clear 'I need your attention' rather than a 'I'm gross and spreading my germs' cough.

"Easton, my office please." Brady bellowed from across the office.

Carly nudged me, hard enough for me to wobble off of my swivel seat, "Mr. Brady's birthday surprise... cheeky." She winked.

I rolled my eyes in return, "I'd be lucky if it's remotely positive." I got up, trudging up the stairs and into his office where his presence was immediately looming over me.

"Take a seat." He gestured to the empty chair on the other side of his desk.

I took it, a bead of sweat instantly breaking out in his intimidating presence. Miles Brady, my cold, emotionless boss.

"Can I help you, Brady?" I shuffled in my seat, leaning back to try and seem more confident than I felt.

"Well, there's no easy way to go around this so...You're fired." He said, monotonously.

"I'm sorry. I'm sorry, what?" My jaw dropped open in complete shock.

"You're fired. Dismissed. Whatever you want to call it, Easton."

"Brady, I don't understand. Have I done something wrong?" My posture shot up like a lightning bolt went right through my spine.

He cleared his throat, shuffling through the tedious amounts of stacks of papers scattered across his desk, finally laying a folder in front of him.

"The decision has been determined that Miss Ellie Easton-Moore will no longer reside as a part of the homicide detective department, on this basis of complications and concerns surrounding psychological wellbeing as of the 15<sup>th</sup>August, 2024. To be re-evaluated as of 2027." He recited, tracing his finger along the paper.

A lump formed in my throat, my stomach churning, my brain melting. They can't fire me just because I *freaked out* at one of the crime scenes. Just because I haven't been able to get that *body* out of my head ever since. What happened to three strikes and you're out? There must be something else. There has to be something else. I felt my heart rise up to my throat, a cold shiver running through my body. This is *not* happening.

I quickly stood up, collecting myself and my rapid breaths, storming out of his office door and towards my desk, snatching my bag and a few of my belongings in one swift swoop and heading towards the door.

"Hey wait! Where are you going?" I heard Carly call after me.

I stopped in my tracks, turning back towards her and noticing Brady haunting the corner of my eye. I shot a glance to him, flicking between the beaming smile from Carly and his cold unsympathetic stare, feeling the hairs prick on the back of my neck. It became harder and harder to swallow the knot which was continuously tightening itself in my throat. Can they see my chest heaving? *Get out of here.* Can they see the millions of thoughts rushing through my head?

I barged through the back exit, immediately and frantically searching for my car keys in my bag. The harsh, cool wind hit me round the face, focusing my vision and dragging me back down to reality. Just focus. Just *breathe.* Centre yourself. I'm fine, nothing is wrong.

"Ellie, where are you going?" The same shrill voice repeated from behind me.

"Brady fired me." I muttered, not bothering to turn around and make eye contact.

"What? No way. He doesn't know what he's doing to the team." She ambled towards me enveloping, suffocating me in a hug.

"Please- Carly, stop. I just need to get out of here. I'll see you around, okay?" I finally dragged my keys out of my bag, getting into my car.

For the first time I felt completely and utterly uneasy in my own company. Driving home, my thoughts proceeded to flood my mind. Getting louder and more insistent and aggravated by the word. No amount of music could drown them out, no amount of city bustle or angry road ragers could've silenced her voice from my mind.

*"Kill her"*

An eerie whisper brushed my ear, completely staggering my train of thought and throwing it off the rails. I swerved off the road, smashing the brake and bumping the curb, my chest rising and falling at the speed of a flash. Adjusting my mirror, I peered into the backseat of my car in attempt to identify the girl's voice which echoed from behind me, but nothing. No one. Yet it felt so real. So vivid.

I opened my door to relieve my mind of its stress and worry and got out the car, in attempt to ground myself. My feet led me away from the car, pacing in lines, circles, muttering absolute nonsense to myself, receiving degrading and questioning glances from passers-by. Tears welled in my eyes, wondering what I did to deserve a day so chaotic, so frenzied, and this specific day of all days.

In the moment where I truly believed that it wouldn't get any worse; *the sirens*. Pulling up next to my car, and the one face I would rather die than see right now, stepping out of the car.

My body collapsed to the floor, unable to hold myself up any longer, in an anxious hyperventilation of what my life was about to come to.

"Easton, get up. Let me take you home." His voice blurred alongside my focus. My vision, my consciousness, my control all quickly spiralling, soon disappearing into absolutely nothing, nothing but silence.

"Okay, let's get you up." I felt my body elevate and drop into a comfortable position.

T he flutter of my eyes opening was nothing less than what I could describe as an awakening movie scene. A girl with no clue where she is, how she got there or memory of the day before her. Bewildering.

"Hey, you're up." A sweet voice came floating into the room, "How're you feeling Els?"

I held my head as I sat up, the world rocking as I do so, "Horrible, like someone smacked my head round with a brick." I groaned, "I don't think I even want to remember what happened."

Theo walked round the corner of my bed, sitting by my feet with a glass of water.

"I can't believe they fired me... on my birthday! Like that should be against the law or something." I hid my face in my hands.

"I mean, I'm sure they had valid reasoning behind it?"

"What? He basically called me insane. He should've just committed me straight to the psych ward." I dropped back,

5

letting the mattress and my pillows envelope me in hope to cover this nightmare, smothering my leftover air.

"You're a detective. No one blames you for driving over that bridge." He slowly removed the pillow from my face, tucking a messy strand of hair behind my ear.

He rested his hand on my thigh and I regained composure and sat up, giving him a pouty look. I swung my legs round out of bed, stretching.

"Are you going to be okay tonight? Do you want me to stay? I've ordered food for us, thought we could still make your birth-night a good one." He cleared his throat, chuckling, bringing him back into my attention.

"Yeah, that would be nice actually." I nodded, leaning my head on his shoulder.

We spent the night giggling hysterically about absolutely nothing, eating, drinking and just enjoying each other's company.

"Here, I got this for you." He brought out a neatly wrapped box from his bag, placing it in my hands.

"Oh T, you really didn't have to." I awed at the black box perfectly knotted with a red silk ribbon.

I slowly pulled it apart, the box revealing itself in layers and layers of photos of Theo and I that we've taken over the years of being friends. My heart surged, remembering all of our fond memories together, "This is beautiful. Thank you." I leant forward, wrapping him in a prolonged hug.

"There's another thing. But you can't open it yet." He placed a smaller box on the table beside us, "I can't tell you when, but you'll know when you need to open it. It's for... future us, let's say." He smiled cheerily, his dimples poking out of his cheeks.

I rolled my eyes and laughed, "What's that supposed to mean?"

He just shrugged, shaking his head and sighing satisfactorily.

My heart skipped a beat, the thought of a 'future us', a future us that could possibly be more than we are now. The thought isn't estranged. Theo's *always* made it very aware of his feelings towards me, on top of the respect he portrays at the fact that I'm simply not ready to make that step with him, but who knows what the future will hold for us?

# Chapter Two

## ELLIE

Why am I doing this to myself? Dark alleys are never *ever* the option. The horribly eerie drips and the deafening silence which almost turned into screams in the misty echoes. With every footstep, every pace, echoed an agonising, heart wrenching dread which filled the emptiness of the alley. What am I even doing here? How did I even get here?

A subtle splash came from the opposing end of the street, stopping me completely in my tracks.

"Hello?" *That was stupid.* The one thing they teach you in horror movies, don't call out *hello* or *who's there* when you're completely alone, and scared nonetheless.

A scream. A real scream. Not the silence turned loud or the echoey drips, a real-life scream. Screaming my name. Screaming for help. The desperation aided my immediate reaction was to run straight towards the sound, sprinting without a second thought to contradict logic.

A hooded figure appeared crouched in front of me, staring right in my direction yet remaining faceless.

Whilst turning away, another lifeless figure came into sight, a young girl, her eyes... her eyes were gone. Bloody. Lifeless on the floor. Recoiling immediately yet remaining frozen to my spot, I felt the bile rising through my stomach up to my throat.

Only to be startled awake by the exact same feeling bringing me to reality and forcing its way out of my body.

I shot straight up, completely drenched in a cold sweat, practically choking on my own air yet still unable to get a breath in. My first instinct was to immediately look at the time. *3:59.* I could still hear her tormenting yells of my name. Her begging for mercy and forgiveness. The number 20 repeating itself, ingrained in my brain as if to tell me or warn me about something. Surely it meant nothing. Surely it was just a dream and it had no deeper meaning at all. It was just a nightmare and I'm just spooked. Nothing at all to worry about. Yet, no matter how hard I try to convince myself, the thoughts and worries brew deeper in my brain until it overflowed into my physicality. Choking me.

I stood up, just blindly walking, out my front door, round corners and corners for God knows how long for. As long as I was panicking and stressing, my feet were moving, my brain was freezing, unable to comprehend or focus on anything that I was doing in this given moment. It was like a trance. I don't remember the path I took, or where I went, or when I got home or when I was cradled into Theo's arms on the cold night floor and if he had tried to come and find me. It's almost as if I was running from the dream, trying to convince myself that that's all it was, but ended up right back where it started.

A trance was all it was. A nightmare.

. . .

T blinked and 3 hours flew by. Last thing I remember was Theo consoling me after my nightmare, after I disappeared into the midst of night, the next thing I know I'm sat on my sofa, wrapped up with a tea freshly prepared on the coffee table in front of me. It was as if I blinked and it snapped me out of the trance. I blinked and my phone rang aggressively, seemingly so far away but yet the pressure forming in my lap.

Wait.

I scampered off of the sofa and out of my blanket in the direction of my work bag, scrambling through the old files for my work phone.

What does *he* want?

"Good morning, Miss Easton."

"You would think after 4 years of working together, we would be on a first name basis by now, huh, Brady." I choked on my words, my voice still croaky, speaking as sarcastically as I could to be reciprocated with a brief pause and a sigh.

"Miss Easton, if you could stop by the office today and return your badge, supplied work phone and to sign your release form, preferably within the next few hours, thank you." He spoke.

"Yeah, you gave me plenty of notice at the ripe time of 7am, thank you very much."

Without another murmur I was hung up on.

I grabbed my purse, sifting through the endless number of cards and different forms of ID's pulling out my police badge and shoving it into my jogger's pocket, grabbing my coat and running my hands through my hair to make myself look somewhat presentable.

Just as I swung open my door to take today in my stride, I almost collapsed into Theo who was holding two coffees and a pastry bag.

"My God, you scared me." I jumped back, startled.

"Where are you going?" He questioned, taking a step inside and balancing the coffees on the edge of the entrance table.

"Brady called, I need to go back to the station and drop the rest of my stuff off." I gestured to my badge and work phone stuffed into my pockets.

"Okay, I'll take you. Let's go." He said, picking up our coffees again and trudging back towards his car.

"Do you want to talk about last night? Or not." He huffed, breaking the silence in the car.

"I just- I just had this really awful dream last night, I'm a bit on edge."

"Ooh, awful huh? Tell me about it." He smiled, laughing as if this were a joke.

"Theo, I'm being serious, it was all gruesome and sickening, this little girl was murdered. She had... her eyes pulled out." I felt my stomach churning in the same motion I felt as if I had just woken up again.

"Gross Els, are you sure that's not just one of the cases you guys solved?" He removed his hand from mine and focused back on the road.

"I'm almost a million percent sure, I definitely would remember if something like that...someone like that was a real case."

I sighed, turning my attention out the window, watching the world go by. Feeling as if there's something so much bigger than a dream just to be ignored. Maybe Brady was right after all, I do need psychological help. Dreaming about little girls with their eyes gouged out can't be normal. It *isn't* normal.

As we sped down the road quickest to get to the station, an element of familiarity flashed right before my eyes.

"Stop! Stop the car Theo. Pull over!" Theo immediately slammed the brakes, reacting to the sheer panic in my voice.

"What?! What's wrong with you?"

Without even acknowledging his words, I swung open the door and began pacing back a few streets, trying to grasp that feeling once again. Through streets and roads of unfamiliarity, I finally stumbled upon the shock horror of my déjà vu, followed by the sounds of Theo yelling my name.

I came to a halt. Freezing, unwillingly unable to move.

"What is it? Is this what you stopped for?" Theo caught up to me, audibly out of breath.

"This, this is it, this is where the murder happened Theo. I know how crazy I sound right now but I promise you it's exactly the same. She was right here and the-the killer was-"

He was silent for a while as I frantically paced the alley, "You mean...your dream? Your dream was in this exact alley? Els, half the alleyways in London look like this." He scoffed, shaking his head.

"No. No, I know how this sounds. I know, okay? Please just believe me, I-I know this is it, this is the one."

"It's probably just déjà vu." He ran his hands over his head.

"No. No Theo. I know-"

"Okay and so it is! What should we do now? Sit around and wait for the murderer to show up?" He raised his voice, his temper overflowing out of him.

He was mocking me. He didn't believe me. *I* wouldn't believe me if I heard the delusions coming out of my own mouth. He's right. This is stupid.

"Fine. You're right. I'm sorry, I'm just shaken up. Let's just go." I ambled my way back to the car, the rest of the drive enveloped in silence.

. . .

As we pulled into the back entrance of the station, still remaining in silence, I grew anxious to walk into the office again. Only to relive all the pity and sympathy looks, and of course the one harsh cold expression too. His presence was intimidating to say the least, even more so that I'm no longer in his good books... as if I ever were.

"I'll wait here." Theo said, distracted with something on his phone. I silently nodded, stepping out the car and making my way straight towards Brady's office.

There was an eerie silence in the office today, time had struck 8am and normally there'd be people crowding around the coffee machine, sorting loose files from last night's case, slagging off Miles Brady in the communal care room. But nothing. Not a soul apart from lonely Mr. Brady sat with his head heavily hung in his hands at his desk. I managed to walk close enough to startle him out of his misery and be greeted with a frustrated sigh.

"Well good morning to you too, grumpy." I rolled my eyes, dropping my badge, phone and a few loose files in front of him.

He sighed, again, running his hands over his eyes and through his dishevelled black hair.

"You look like you haven't slept since...well, since you fired me. Need some help with that?" I pointed to the case file which had formed on his desk which would usually go through my desk first.

He pushed a piece of paper towards me alongside a pen, without so much as lifting his head to look at me.

Just as quickly as I signed it, he spoke up, "You can leave now." Miserably.

I sighed, I genuinely couldn't get anywhere with him and that was my last chance trying.

. . .

13

"**D**id everything go okay?" Theo looked over to me before pulling out of the car park, noticing my deep sigh and hunched posture as I re-entered the car.

"Yeah, just Brady being an absolute troll as per." He laughed at my pathetic excuse of an insult.

Clearing his throat immediately after, a silence dropped between us, interrupted by quiet exhales on his behalf. As we came to a stop by a red light, Theo dramatically turned his body towards me, placing a hand on my knee.

"Els, I'm sorry if it came out as if I was mocking you, I- I just... it's a little hard to believe you know? I'm on your side I promise, I was just confused and didn't know how to react and clearly, I reacted in the wrong way I just," He rambled on. And on. *And on.* He tripped and stuttered over his words trying to apologise a million times a second, profusely telling me how much he didn't mean it and how much he didn't mean it and how he's sorry and how much he didn't mean it.

"Theo, stop talking. It's fine, you're forgiven." I held his hand, still resting on my knee and squeezed it. I notice flick between his eyes being on the road and on my hand multiple times, like he also felt the jolt of electricity from our contact.

# Chapter Three

## ELLIE

"Come on, it won't be that bad. Stop being such a party pooper!" She squealed down the telephone line, making my ear ring.

Carly has been trying to convince me to come to the monthly staff club night for the last 20 minutes and I'm not giving in and saying yes.

"Carls, I don't even work with you guys anymore. I can't come to a work party." I sighed. The truth is I actually wouldn't mind going, it's not the people or the idea of clubbing in general.

"Fine. Then call it an impromptu post-birthday bash, with all your best *amigas*!" She sang.

Carly is *always* bursting and bubbling with energy. Sometimes she gets too excited, or even sometimes, when she's angry or just feeling a lot of emotions in general, she'll burst into fluent Spanish. She's like a shaken-up champagne bottle with the cork popped off. Just bubbles exploding everywhere.

"Okay. Okay! I'll come. Where are we meeting?" I gave in, laughing at her excitement.

"Yes! You won't regret it I promise. Parker's designated driver so he'll pick us up and drop us home." I could hear how wide her grin was right now.

*Parker.* Of course, of all people to be the sober sitter for a work party it had to be the guy I.... well, *we* had a thing, in my first year of working with the team. There's never been any awkwardness or bad blood, it's just the reason that anything even started in the first place was because of all these drunk nights out with the team.

"Where'd you go? I lost you for a second there." Her tone quietened down.

"Sorry, just thinking about what I was going to wear." I'm a terrible liar in person. Everyone knows that, over the phone, people can't see the signs, it's easier to lie.

"Okay, I'll pick you up at 9? We'll do drinks at mine and then Parker will come and get us at half 10." She set out the plan for the evening, sounding impossibly more excited than she did before.

"Alright, see you at 9." I hung up, standing completely silently still for a moment, wondering what I got myself into.

Realising the time is 7:30 already, I poured myself a vodka tonic and took the tequila out of the cupboard as a reminder to bring it to Carly's and hit shuffle on my playlist.

*Beyoncé* comes on and immediately I've gotten in the mood to go out clubbing with them. Music can weirdly change a mood, one minute I'm dreading going out, the next I'm choreographing a whole dance in the shower while switching between *Fergie* and *Will.i.am's* vocals. I also know for a fact if any one of Lizzy McAlpine or Adele's come on shuffle, I'll be on the floor of my shower sobbing within seconds.

Within 3 minutes, *Maneater* by *Nelly Furtado* comes on, and I seriously debate having a concert shower for the rest of the night rather than going out. Before I convince myself that's the better idea, I get out, wrapping one towel around my body and wrapping one around my hair, shimmying my way to my room.

I grab my makeup bag and sit down on the floor in front of my full length and start doing a subtle glam look with 5-minute dance breaks in between every mini step.

"Ellie Baby!! I missed you." Carly attacked me in hugs and peppered kisses.

"I saw you 4 days ago!" I chuckled, repeating her same high-pitched squeal as her, returning the hug nonetheless.

"Well, aren't you just a sexy bag of bones." She eyed me up and down, biting her lip exaggeratedly.

"Not too bad yourself." I winked back at her dramatically and walked into her house.

"I have to tell you something." She immediately turned serious after shutting her front door.

My heart dropped, secretly knowing that she's joking around but still nervous about what she has to say.

"Parker's actually the one who begged me to beg you to come. Like obviously I want you there too but he was all like *"Please convince Ellie, she'll listen to you."* She mocked his tone extremely accurately.

My jaw dropped open, admittedly more dramatic than I would like to admit, "Oh, I don't think I can be friends with you anymore. That's just horrific." I threw my hand to my forehead and shook my head dramatically, resulting in a deep witchy cackle from Carly.

"Who knows, maybe you'll end up deep in the Park-ing

space." She winked, giving me finger guns, alongside her terrible pun that was enough to make me want to go home.

Instead, I whipped out the bottle of tequila from my bag, "Shots?" I beamed at her, her immediately nodding enthusiastically.

T couldn't see wonky. Straight? The room was *spinning* around me, or... just me spinning in circles. It was nice to be absolutely carefree for once. Not having to worry about what they think about me because I'm not in this godforsaken team anymore.

"Aren't you glad you came?" I closed my eyes, giving into the drift of the tequila swaying through my system, leaning my head against Carly's shoulder who I was currently dancing with.

"Mhm." I nodded, smiling at her.

I noticed her break eye contact with me and fall out of rhythm with our two-step hip sway and look over my shoulder.

It took absolutely all of the minimal sobriety left in me to not follow her glance, "Who is it?" I whisper shouted into her ear.

"See for yourself! You've got *all* of his attention." She had a cheesy, giddy grin planted on her face.

I spun my head around, the room moving in slow motion as I did so, my vision focusing on one man staring in my direction in particular. Miles Brady. Leaning against the wall with a scotch on the rocks swirling in his hand. He was making unforgiving, dead eye contact with me, not threatening to break it anytime soon with a taunting smile on his face.

"Go and talk to him *amorcito*! You've obviously piqued his

interest." Carly nudged me, albeit a lot harder than she probably intended, causing me to stumble over my own two feet slightly.

A newfound, unknown, sudden confidence washed over me, immediately surging me towards him.

"So, you do smile?" I barely managed to keep myself upright, a wave of nervousness dawning on me from suddenly being in his presence.

"Only if I see something worthy of smiling at." His tongue ran over his bottom lip and the aura of alcohol enveloped us both. He leant forward, his hot breath brushing against my ear, "And you, *Easton*, are definitely worth smiling for. *You always have been.*" His last words absolutely knocked my knees out of place, causing them to wobble slightly. I gripped onto his already loose tie, keeping the close distance between us.

His expression faltered, flicking between a pleasurable, careless and confused, regretting expression.

He pulled away slightly, staying mere inches away from my face with that taunting, gorgeous smile. My gaze dropped to the small gap in between our bodies, glazing over my hand holding his tie and the necklace dangling down the front of my dress.

"My eyes are up here, *Trouble*." The corner of his lip turned up as he shook his head and tutted his t's.

My breath hitched in my throat, as I didn't even think my knees could get any weaker, he writhed a hand round my waist, pulling me even closer so that I could feel his heart thumping against mine through our chests. His eyes glanced to my lips as his arm snaked off my back and he downed the rest of his drink in one.

"Ellie?!" I swung my head round, recognising the familiar excited voice.

"Hey Parker," I gleamed, turning my body away from Brady and taking a step, falling towards Parker. I felt a brush on my shoulder, turning around to see Brady speeding away through the crowd.

I rolled my eyes at his constant change in demeanour and slung my arms around Parker's shoulders, swaying to the music which had slowed down a bit.

"Hi gorgeous," His sultry voice resonated through my ears, "Have I told you that you look absolutely amazing tonight?" He looked me up and down, smiling slightly and biting his lip.

"You have. At Carly's...in the car on the way here...when you bought me my drink..." I flicked my hair over my shoulder, pulling him closer to me, "You can tell me again though." I whisper-shouted in his ear.

"You look amazing. Stunning." He cleared his throat, flustered.

He held my waist firmly, running his thumbs over my hips, a smile tugging on his lips.

"Want to get out of here? It's quite stuffy." I started fanning myself, pulling my hair up into a ponytail, holding it with my hand.

He nodded frantically with a wide smile on his face, snaking an arm round my waist and tagging along behind me.

Saying the most outrageous thing that I can think of just to taunt him while he was driving back to my house while in a hazy drunk, half sober state was easier than I make it sound. Or maybe Parker's just easy to taunt.

"Come on." I instantly got out the car as he turned the engine off, skipping to my front door with him right on my tail. As I struggled slightly with the keys in the front door he snaked his hands around my waist, placing a kiss on my cheek, then my shoulder.

I swung the door open and almost immediately as I walked in, the lamp across the room switched on. It was almost an exact replication of a scene in those movies where the teenagers get caught sneaking in with a boy late from a party and their parents sitting all ominously in the corner on that one random sofa? Except it wasn't a parent, it was Theo. He stunned me in my tracks, Parker half hanging on my shoulder and my weight slung over his arm.

I tried to adjust myself so I wasn't completely relying on him to hold me up and plastered a smile on my face, "Theo, what're you doing here? I told you I was going out." I untangled myself from Parker and hobbled towards the sofa, flopping onto it and almost missing it completely.

"I got worried, you weren't answering your phone, so I thought I'd just make sure you got home safe." I'm not sure when but he got up from his position and was now crouched in front of me, stroking the hair out of my face.

"I... should go?" Parker's voice re-entered my foggy brain.

"No."

"Yes."

Theo and I spoke simultaneously, exchanging glances with each other and then back to Parker.

"I'll call you." Parker cleared his throat before stepping out the door.

I sat up, now face to face with Theo, shooting him a moody look and pouting.

"What?" He smiled.

"You need to stop turning up here without me knowing." I stood up, feeling overwhelmingly sick and heading over to the kitchen to grab a glass of water.

"Isn't that why you gave me a spare key?" I didn't even have to look at him to know he was giving me a smug look, "So it wasn't for our weekly horror movie nights?" I heard the frown form on his lips.

I ignored him, not wanting to have to deal with his form of attitude. Undoubtedly, it's most likely the weight of the alcohol dragging over my shoulder but I'm finding it *increasingly* hard to tolerate him right now.

"I'll be on the sofa if you need me." He yelled toward me as I ambled to my bedroom, flipping him off behind my back, without turning around again.

# *Chapter Four*

## ELLIE

Getting home at 3 and still being awake at half 3 was a complete shock to me considering I was ready to pass out in the car on the way home. I sat up in bed, not knowing why I was so suddenly awake. I glanced at the clock, and then to my phone, realising the time and date.

The time switched from 3:59 to 4am, the 20th August, which I would love to convince myself was a coincidence, considering that was exactly the date and time that my nightmare took place, and that *can't* be a coincidence that I'm suddenly unable to sleep. The days completely merging into one definitely did not help my anxiety surrounding the number 20, the date. The only reason I forgot about it is because Carly dragged me out tonight and time just completely flew by. The 20th had finally rolled around and after wallowing in my own self-pity for 3 days I was stuck in an endless cycle of sweaty palms and pacing around my bedroom. I was definitely stressing myself out for no reason at all, it was just a dream and I was psyching myself out because who knows why. I'll be fine. If I just meditate, everything will go away, I'll trick myself to be tired and it'll be good. No. Every time I close my eyes, I can see *her*. *Her* eyes. The cycle of words fumbling around my head. Kill her. Kill her. Kill her. No. I was safe in my own bed and-

Nothing is happening.

I ran to the bathroom, splashing my face with cold water in attempt to regain control of my thoughts, become less agitated, less frantic. I stared at my unrecognisable reflection, her staring right back. I could've sworn she grinned at me, she was distorted, a face no longer my own appearing over me. The distant clock ticking and chiming engraved into my thoughts, the distant sound of Theo's snore echoing down the hall into my mind. Almost as if she was letting me know it was almost time. Almost time. The time.

I ambled back over to my bedside, turning the clock face down, out of my eyeline. Surely this is just my panicked mind playing tricks on me, this paranoia is way too much to handle and all because of a stupid dream. I need to drive, walk, do anything other than stay in this tight room.

I quickly grabbed my keys and strode through the hallway, my heavy breaths immediately waking Theo up.

"Where are you going?" I fiddled with the keys, my hands trembling making it 10 times harder.

"Out. I need to get out of here." My voice, just as shaky as my hands.

"You've drunk a lot; I don't think that's smart Els." He stood up, yawning and hobbling over to me. Just as he got close to me, I managed to slip out of the door and run into my car, immediately starting the engine and swerving off the front drive.

My eyes focused on everything but the road, little side alleys, weird bumps in the road, anything suspicious or out of sight. Everything, and I mean *everything* looked out of place at around 4 am.

Something on the floor of the passenger side caught my eye in a glimmer. I leant down, still gripping the steering wheel at full speed to hold my balance. I just... couldn't...reach-

A loud bang, and my whole body jolting forward.

My head flew against the front of the passenger side's glove compartment.

I tried to lift my head up, immediately getting hit with a wave of dizziness and blurry spells. I couldn't even see what happened. I could've sworn I heard screams in the distance, but not one bit of my consciousness could stay focused enough to do anything to help.

Only instead of fading out of my field of hearing, the further unconscious I got, the screaming got louder, and louder, screaming at the top of her lungs. As if the sound was repeating on a stuck record, scratched by her clawing at me for help.

And silence.

Nothing but silence.

Whether the sunlight gleaming through my window woke me up or the aggressive, *aggravating*, brash knocking on my front door, I was startled awake. I slammed the pillow into my face, muffling my groan. Maybe if I ignore it, it'll go away.

I sat up reluctantly, noticing a note from Theo placed strategically on the coffee table in front of me.

The coffee table? Meaning, I'm not in my bed. My head immediately started pounding from the copious amounts of tequila, that I will never be ingesting on that level ever again.

The continued banging on the front door is *not* making this in any way better.

I groggily stood up, rubbing my eyes, trying to bring my feet back down to reality and sulked towards the door.

Before even slightly cracking open my front door, a harsh push made me stumble back, catching my balance on my kitchen counter.

"Would you so kindly like to tell me what you're doing *bursting into my house?*" I stood up, folding my arms and shaking my head.

How dare he fire me, then barge into my house and then-

"I need to talk to you. It's an emergency." He shut the door behind him, looking out the window as if he were some kind of fugitive.

"Okay, if you've become some kind of criminal and you're on the run, I'm gonna have to ask you to leave, effective immediately." I held my hands up in surrender.

"You need to shut up." He turned to face me; an angry scolding look planted on his face.

"Don't come into *my* house, and tell *me* to shut up, Brady." I took a step towards him.

"You're going to need to tell me why your car was crashed right next to the scene of a crime this morning. Effective immediately." He mocked me, glaring into my soul. If looks could kill? I'd be dead and gone. Six feet under.

"What?" I stuttered, confused, but hazily starting to slowly remember the previous night. Oh my God. *Oh my God.* I looked at Brady, immediately having to look away after getting a flood of memories from our encounter at the work outing, "I- uh, I don't remember.... anything, from last night." I stumbled my words out, still avoiding eye contact with him.

I picked up the note on the table, quickly giving it a quick scan before shoving it into my pocket, shooting my glance back to Brady.

***Just going to pick up your car, back soon. -T***

What if he got arrested? What if he got there and the murder happened and they were all over him and they thought that he was trying to remove evidence and... and he was going to jail for the rest of his life because of me and I'm a horrible friend because now it seems like I've framed him, or what's worse. Oh my God.

"Where's Theo?" I frantically spun to face him, pacing over and standing my ground in front him.

"I'm asking the questions here, Easton." He gritted his teeth at me.

"No. I'm not letting him get framed for murder. I can't do that to him- I can't do that to"

"Murder?" He interrupted, "And how do you know that detail?" He took a step towards me.

My mouth went completely dry. How on earth was I meant to spin myself out of this one? It felt as if someone was hammering against my chest at the rate my heart was pounding.

"Easton." He took a step closer, with his presence didn't help my nerves and panic. His demeanour was so strong, over-whelming, intimidating, it's almost like he pulled the words out of my mouth himself.

"A couple nights ago I had this vision that a girl was murdered in an alley down the road near the station and she had her eyes pulled out and I've been so nervous ever since I had it because for some reason today's date has been stuck in my head and it just felt more like reality than a stupid dream or vision or–"

I quickly realised I was rambling and hadn't taken a breath since, well since he walked in my house.

He looked stunned, for once in his entire life he looked

taken off guard, like he didn't know what to do. He stumbled around his pockets, almost remorsefully bringing out a pair of handcuffs.

"I really hoped you had a good explanation for this Easton but I'm gonna have to arrest you. You're under arrest for suspicion of association with manslaughter, you..." He began reciting my rights and cautions.

"No. Brady, please." I begged, fighting against him slightly.

He clipped the handcuffs round my wrists, creating a firm grasp on my arms, pulling me into his clutch, "Don't make this any harder for me, Easton." His coarse voice brushed against my ear sending a tingle up my spine.

His voice against my ear sent a flashback through my mind of last night. I shook my head, trying to get back into reality but not succeeding with his grip tight against my wrists. I was getting arrested; this was absolutely it for me and my newfound freedom. There was no way to prove I was innocent, nor guilty but who am I to prove that?

***

"Can I get a coffee or something please?" I yelled through the hollow, echoey room, only allowing me to see myself through the blurry haze reflecting back at me.

Almost instantly, my ex-superior, Brady's boss, Agent Prescott walked in, side by side with Brady. He stayed by the door, purposefully avoiding eye contact with me whilst Prescott took a seat in front of me.

"Miss Easton, I would say it's a pleasure but considering the circumstances..." He leant forward on the table condescendingly.

"So... that's a no to the coffee?" I smiled out of pure nerves, not even meaning to portray it.

"I'm going to get right to the point here, Ellie. Agent Brady over there has reported back that he's found concrete evidence against you at the scene of the crime. Not only that but you knew details about our victim without them even being published to the media. Care to explain yourself?"

The feeling begun to rise through my body again. The nausea, the paranoia, the fear and distrust of myself.

"Sir, you have to listen to me because this is going to sound ridiculous, okay?" He nodded, gesturing for me to continue, "I had a... vision, a dream, about the exact details of the murder, as if I witnessed it first-hand." He rolled his eyes immediately. "A few days ago, Agent Brady asked me to come in and hand in my badge, and on the way, I passed the alley. It freaked me out so I went to look if there was anyone there, but no one was. I must have subconsciously driven there last night, I don't know, I promise I have nothing to do with...it."

He sighed, exchanging looks between me and Brady, "Where were you last night Ellie?"

"I-I was at home, after the party, the whole night, apart from the drive...of course" I grew anxious, knowing the feeling of time speeding by. The more I talked, the more guilty I looked. I knew they weren't believing a single word that I said. Knowing that I blacked out and woke up in my home like nothing happened? It's not true though, I was just in a haze, panicked.

"And were you at home alone?"

Panic. "No. I was with my best friend. Theodore Grey. He left at about 6 this morning because he has work and so I went back to sleep and was woken up by Agent Brady at 8." Too many details. Why did I lie to the police? It's true of course that

I was with him but God knows when he actually left for work, if he's in jail right now, if he got my car or...

"Theodore Grey is next door, telling us the exact same story. Word. For. Word."

"So why did we find him near your car at the scene of the crime this morning?"

"He wanted to bring my car home just so it wasn't just...on the street, I think?"

There was an eerie silence held, making me increasingly nervous by the second. Without breaking eye contact, Prescott began smiling sadistically at me, like he was enjoying this?

"Tell me about your night, you watch a movie?"

"No, I was out with the work team. I barely talked to him when I got home." I looked down, my leg reflexively bouncing under the table.

"Did you go home alone?" He pressed.

"Yes." An invisible hand wrapped around my throat, choking me out, my leg bouncing out of control. I would rather say anything than drag any more people into this.

"So not only did you crash, and are aware of the crime scene, you were drunk-driving, yes?" He stared me down.

"Yes." I swallowed, my breath completely escaping me.

Prescott cleared his throat, nodding "And where did Theo sleep?" Prescott pulled out a small pocket notebook, scribbling down every word. Tactic. It's something we do to make the suspect nervous, and my god it is working.

"He slept on my sofa."

"And where does Mr. Grey work?"

"He owns a restaurant further into town. He's head chef."

"Interesting, and you say he left at 6? Correct me if I'm wrong but it takes over an hour to get into town from your address, no?"

"Just about 50 minutes, Sir."

Silence.

"Thank you, Ellie." He stood up, retreating out of the room as quickly as he entered.

"Wait, how long am I going to be here for?" I attempted to walk after him, being pulled back down by the handcuffs shackled to the table.

More silence. They're making me go insane. More than usual if anything.

I need to get out of here. The most they can hold me for is 72 hours and that's without evidence, maybe even more with the drinking and driving. What're the chances of this? I lied on the most law-abiding, honest man to ever exist in this entire world. Just my luck.

Less than 30 minutes later, a stern look attracted my attention through the stained glass on the holding room door. Theo followed by Agent Prescott glared at me, only one with a sadistic smirk planted on his face. The pair then trailed in front of Agent Brady who briefly paused by the door to my room, before sighing and stepping in, shutting the door behind him.

He exhaled, closing his eyes and shaking his head before taking a seat in front of me. I stayed quiet, knowing that me speaking wouldn't do much to help my case right now. He tapped his fingers together, clutching them 3 inches away from mine. He went to say something, giving me a hopeless yet longing look, stopping himself and sighing.

"You're gonna wear your heart out if you keep sighing, you know." I joked, in an attempt to break the silence, only to be returned with... a weak smile? A smile nonetheless, "He smiles!" I feel like the second I said that we both finally acknowledged last night, without a word but a mutual understanding that we will *never* talk about it.

His smile disappeared just as quickly as it had formed,

finally going into his words, "I really don't want to keep you here Easton."

"Then send me home Brady, I didn't do it I swear. I know that doesn't mean anything but you know me. I've been in your team for 4 years; I wouldn't do this." I pleaded. He broke eye contact with me the second I said his name, sighing. *Again.*

"Your psych eval-"

"I'm not crazy." I forcibly interrupted.

"Please just listen to me, Easton. Your psych eval spiked in many areas. You were a valuable asset to our team and that will always be remembered. But right now, I am fighting against Prescott for *your* sake and God knows why I am and everything and everyone is telling me to stop." He gritted his teeth.

Something was wrong. Very wrong. He wasn't being himself, his *usual* self. He wasn't being aggressive, or cold or arrogant, he was helping me?

"I'm doing everything in my power to let you go. I know you lied about *something* because I know you. I know that your leg bounces like crazy when you tell a lie, and I know that Prescott couldn't see that from where he was sitting. Now if Mr. Grey tells the truth or something remotely different from your story, you're getting arrested and there is nothing I will be able to do about that, but if he lies on your behalf... I know nothing." He held up his hands in a surrendering motion.

"Why are you doing this? All this time, I thought you hated me." I shook my head, completely confused by this new light he's shone upon himself.

"I'm a very private person, Miss Easton." He went to continue his sentence before a harsh bang on the door inter-rupted him, startling us both.

Agent Prescott stormed into the room, not letting the door shut behind him, gesturing his head from Brady towards me and nodding.

Brady gets up, ruffling through his pockets and bringing out a key and unlocking my handcuffs, "We'll take you somewhere that you can stay for the night." He mumbled, avoiding any eye contact with me.

"I have to stay?" I struggled against his strong grasp on my wrists as he guided me out of the interrogation room and followed Prescott down the steps to the holding cell.

Thrown into the cell, disregarded for the night, left alone with my thoughts and the darkness which slowly crept in, an exact replica of these thoughts invading my mind.

# Chapter Five

## ELLIE

"You're free to go." A harsh clang startled me awake, jolting me upright.

The night flew by. As much as I couldn't sleep, as much as the thoughts of the visions repeatedly invaded my head and the idea that I could potentially be stuck here for an indefinite amount of time haunted me.

Prescott glared at me through the rusty metal bars, scolding me as I got up and stalked towards him, stretching.

"I told you I was innocent." I coughed under my breath, slightly barging against his shoulder on my way past.

He retorted, harshly grabbing my arm, "I'll prove you guilty, trust me." His grasp tightened, leaving a purple forming bruise wrapped around my wrist.

Theo and Brady came walking round the corner, Theo glaring daggers in my direction and Agent Brady glancing between myself and Agent Prescott, slowing nodding.

I cleared my throat, taking a step away from Prescott and towards Theo, making pleading eye contact with him, knowing he was about to give me a world's worth of words on the journey home.

"You know I don't do this shit Ellie. If you get me in trouble with the law, you're taking the fall. I have done way too well for myself to let your stupid visions ruin my life." He spat with nothing but pure annoyance, hitting his palms against the steering wheel.

"Look, I know I screwed up, okay? It's not like I don't have a life to ruin too. I told you I was sorry, what more do you want from me?" I ran my hands through my hair, trying not to let the tears pooling in my eyes overflow. I looked out the window, biting my lip to stop myself from saying another word, to stop the knot in my throat from tightening any more.

"You don't have a job, Ellie. You stay at home every day and you're gonna have crazy murderous dreams that you think are going to come true. You need to stop with this, it's only going to get you into more trouble and quite frankly, I won't be landing myself in jail with you again." He continued to ramble on and on about how crazy I was and how successful and amazing his life was and pretty much how he doesn't need someone like me to ruin it again.

I get it. I messed up. But he doesn't need to degrade me to what I already know is the truth about the difference between the two of us.

I immediately got out of the car the second that he pulled up to my house, my shaky hands not managing to quickly grab my keys, only to be welcomed by the sound of the car door opening and closing yet again.

"I'm sorry Els. I'm just upset, I don't mean it." I felt his two gentle yet firm hands snake around my waist, restricting me and pulling me back towards him.

His grasp was so warm but so conflicted. So acquainted yet unfamiliar. So familiar but discomforting. I felt my physicality leaning further into him seeking the familiar comfort, but my consciousness wondering what I really wanted or not. He was always here, always. He saved my life, and has saved it multiple times by just being him. But is he what I wanted? What I needed? What I needed was stability and maybe I'm confused between someone who's been with me all my life and something I've needed all my life. Someone who makes me feel like dirt at the bottom of his shoe one minute and the most important person in the world the next.

Composing myself, I finally pulled myself away from Theo, taking a breath and brushing his touch off of me, "I'll see you soon, okay?" I nodded, smiling lightly and going into my door, leaving him standing hopeless outside.

He stops the door closing with his foot, just before I shut it.

"I feel awful, let me make you dinner." He had a sweet, pleading smile on his face that I just couldn't resist or say no to.

I nodded, reopening the door and allowing him to step in.

He immediately rushed to the kitchen, grabbing his designated apron and washing his hands. I stood, taking in his presence, simply just staring, admiring. As hot-headed as he can be, at the end of the day, I do understand his anger. I would be furious if someone landed me in jail for the night for something we didn't do.

"Can I ask you something?" He spoke up after a few minutes of silence.

I nodded, humming in approval.

"Would you ever take up therapy? Not that I don't want to help you, I just feel like I *can't* and maybe it would be good to talk to a professional about your... dreams. I really think you should. And I don't want to come across as bossy. Because I'm not bossy. I'm just...being...assertive." He shrugged, turning his back to face me and slowly stirring the pot on the stove.

I remained silent for a second, trying to comprehend what he suggested. As if he's even tried to help me at all, he'd rather send me into therapy like I'm some kind of lunatic, just for them to judge me too.

"What use would it be?" I leant against the counter, pushing my head into my hands.

I felt a pair of hands envelope mine, bringing them away from my face and kissing them gently, "You never know unless you try."

I nodded, biting my bottom lip and making solid eye contact with him, "Okay, I'll try it."

A smile immediately spread on his face, "Thank you. And if it's terrible then you can stop going." He walked round the kitchen counter, pressing his lips to my forehead and lingering there for a moment.

I inhaled, taking in a strong whiff of his cologne and snaking my arms around his waist. Throughout my disapproval of his idea, I know he just wants what is best for me, and who am I to be angry at him for that? He's trying to be the best, best friend he can be by doing or suggesting whatever he can to help me.

N ot even allowing me a second to breathe, my phone pinged with a message notification of a link from Theo. I reluctantly click the link and it directs me to a page with 6 different numbers of therapists within the area. As much as I grudgingly agreed to his *tremendous* idea, what am I even meant to say? *Hi! I'm Ellie and I had a vision about a murder that came true, and guess what! I got arrested for it because somehow the whole case was pointing to me as the main suspect! Smiley face exclamation mark.* He would rather that, than me come to him as my best friend and confide in him my worries and stresses and at least trying to help.

I glance out the window to my drive, noticing him still sitting in his car while on the phone to someone, seemingly frustrated or upset. I close the blinds before he notices me looking and sit down on the sofa, bringing out my laptop and pulling up the same website. If this is the only way that Theo is not going to call me crazy and stupid then so be it, maybe he's right after all, maybe this is the best option for me. Getting my mind sifted through by a judgmental middle-aged woman who sits in a chair scribbling away in a notebook is not my ideal idea of a fun evening.

I land on the profile of the first woman suggested on the website, 'Angela Swildens, 45, expert in her profession of mental health and amazing clientele. Associated with multiple children's and animal charities'- *Next.* A person who writes about themselves in third person bragging about how many charities they support and how many people they've helped when that is their literal job is not someone that I want to be spending my evenings with.

I sift through different options, my interest and willingness to do this decreasing more and more with every profile that I read.

Until I came across Dr. Harley Taylor. Her picture was cute, it was her standing in a field of daisies with a puppy golden retriever in her hand. She had curlyish, frizzy auburn hair and a big, cheesy, wild grin on her face. I immediately liked her because even just her profile picture made her seem like a normal person. It wasn't a business shot or a passport photo but just her being herself. *'Here to listen and advise. Not to judge'* alongside a few fun facts about herself was her profile and I instantly decided to email her, asking for a trial session and when her next availability was and within an hour, I had gotten a response from her.


T *o Miss Easton-Moore,*
    *Thank you for taking your time to consider my services! I have just had a slot cancelled at midday tomorrow if you're free. I appreciate this is last minute however I am willing to squeeze you in if you are able to make it.*

    *Looking forward to hearing back from you and potentially meeting you tomorrow!*


B *est Wishes,*
    *Dr. Harley Taylor.*

# *Chapter Six*

ELLIE

"It's a pleasure to be able to meet you in person so quickly, Miss Moore." I shook hands with Dr. Taylor, a precious, welcoming smile spread across her face.

"It's lovely to meet you too, and I prefer Easton if that's okay. Just Ellie is even better." I made my way over to the sofa, taking a seat and attempting to make myself as comfortable as possible in said circumstances. On a sincere reflection, I'm starting to question why I was ever confused that I was fired on the basis of a mental health crisis concern in the first place. I could barely focus on cases anymore, my mind was just constantly running at a million miles an hour, it was a situation doomed from the very beginning.

"Right, let's just get straight into this, shall we?" She adjusted herself, getting comfortable in her own chair while adjusting the notebook on the table beside her.

"Yeah, yeah okay. Where do you want me to start?" I chuckled, recycling the longitude of events in my life which has led me to this point in time.

"Let's start as recently as you can, and we'll work backwards to what has led you to sitting here today." She nodded.

"Okay, well, I was fired, like, a week ago?" I paused, trying to work out the timeframe of events, "It was my 27th birthday." I sighed, debating how much I wanted to open up to her. Yes, she's my therapist and yes, I really want to trust her. But I don't want to be branded the town's crazy lady. Brady and Prescott definitely already think that, so does Theo even though I'm quite literally only doing this therapy thing *for him,* "I had a rough following hours, very much just completely in my head, panicking, worrying."

"How did you feel at that moment, when they fired you?"

"I was annoyed at him, my boss and... I was annoyed at myself. I was a detective so I feel like I should have been better in hiding myself, healing myself, I shouldn't have let the case get to me as much as it did."

There was a brief silence, an unsaid urge for me to continue, "I had a vision...a premonition, about a crime, that eventually happened and it made me look very guilty."

I tried to be as vague as I possibly could, after all it doesn't sound amazing jumping into the hot seat and immediately waving a big red flag that says I could possibly be a murderer, how fun would that be? No, *I'm not a murderer.* I just happen to not remember anything from that night, no big deal, I know myself, I would never hurt anyone. *I'd never kill anyone.*

"Did you tell anyone about this vision at the time?" She jotted notes down.

"I told my best friend, Theo, he didn't really react in the best way. He thought I was being crazy, he's kind of the reason I'm here today too. I don't want to lose him and I don't think things will ever be the same if I didn't come to therapy." I relaxed back into the chair, letting it engulf me slightly.

"Therapy should be a personal choice; you shouldn't have

to feel like it's a last resort or an option forced onto you as an ultimatum. No matter what you are going through." She looked at me with sympathy, continuing, "So tell me more about Theo. What's your relationship like with him?"

"We've been friends for forever, since we were both...7, I think. There's been times where, well, other people came in between us, or I pushed him away because, well, he's always been very open about having feelings for me and that... scares me. But he's the only constant in my life, so I've always had that to hold on to." I stumbled over my words to try and explain 20 years of friendship in a mere minute, "I would never want to lose him, even thinking about it breaks my heart. It's just, when he called me crazy, it felt like a really personal dig at me. We've never really had arguments or fights but I felt a push of distance between us in that moment."

"Okay..." She scribbled down notes, "Have you made it clear to him that this is not something that you're 100 percent comfortable with?"

I shook my head, "I haven't really talked to him about it, I'm seeing him tonight though. I'll tell him then." I nodded, trying to convince myself that that was what I was going to do.

After 30 minutes more of ranting about my pathetic excuse of a life, time was up, I paid her the fee that we agreed on for a trial session and left, finally letting the cold hair hit my face, breathing after what felt like an entire hour of just holding my breath and walking on eggshells.

I walked across the street, planning on just picking up a takeaway for Theo and I tonight but being startled by someone yelling my name from across the street.

"Ellie? Ellie! Is that you?"

"Olivia? I haven't- wow it's so good to see you." I was instantly greeted with a tight hug from the excitable voice which sprung towards me.

"How are you! You look amazing." She beamed, my dishevelled messy bun and smudged mascara under my eyes *really* supporting her compliment. Instead, she has the neatest, most perfect blonde ponytail, the type you see in hair commercials, with a beautiful bright smile almost permanently pressed onto her face, dressed in the tidiest, most flattering suit I think I've ever seen in my life.

Olivia Charlotte. How to describe Olivia Charlotte? She was our friend in school, Theo's girlfriend, then Theo's ex-girlfriend. She hated me, then we were friends. We were best friends, then we weren't.

"I'm...I'm doing great, I can't believe it's you." She pulled me into her arms again. If you would've told me I'd be running into Olivia Charlotte outside a therapy building while thinking about my relationship with Theo, I would've cried of laughter.

"I know, this is amazing! I would love to stay and chat but I'm actually late for something, we should grab a coffee soon, okay?" She waved, in a way that could only be described as her fingers folding into her palm, almost flapping at me, definitely pretentiously, with a pouty smile as she strutted away.

Almost mesmerised by her aura, I completely missed that she would have no way to keep in contact, yet as I realised, she was already long out of my sight. I sighed heavily to myself, that was like a fever dream, who would've thought.

Olivia Charlotte, if she wanted to get into contact with you, she would find a way. I remember her name appearing in the newspaper a few years ago, the youngest author to publish a textbook less than a year after finishing her degree in law. It was bestselling for 2 years, before she went dark and now has moved to London for law school! Fantastic, some more competition.

*Chapter Seven*

ELLIE

"You'll never guess who I saw today." I almost choked on the mouthful of takeaway that I had previously shoved into my mouth.

Soon after, Theo came and joined me on the sofa, his own takeout box in hand and chopsticks at the ready, "Who?"

Swallowing my food, I turned to face him, sitting cross legged and slapping his arm excitedly, "Olivia Charlotte."

The second the name left my mouth, Theo choked, splattering noodles all over the coffee table.

"Ew, Theo, Gross." I laughed, redirecting my attention to the TV.

"Where did you see her?" He tapped his chopsticks on the side of the box repetitively.

"I bumped into her outside of therapy," I cleared my throat at the mention of the all-taboo subject hoping he would get the hint and change the subject. Of course, he didn't.

"You went? This is going to be so good for you I promise." He grabbed my arm, putting both of our food on the coffee table in front of us and then tackling me in a hug, nuzzling his face into the crease in my neck, "How was it?" He stayed laying on my chest. I removed my hand from being trapped underneath him and threaded my fingers through his hair.

"It was alright, I guess. Nothing out of the ordinary. I liked her a lot, she was nice. She took a lot of notes." I clicked the TV remote, turning the volume up, trying to avoid detailed conversation.

He took the hint this time, nodding and looking between me and the TV, "I'm proud of you, you know. Thanks for giving this a chance." He stood up, giving me back my food. He placed a kiss on the top of my head and headed back towards the kitchen, stunning me and making me freeze mid-chew. That was oddly *comforting*.

"I wonder when she came back to town." I reverted the subject back to Olivia. Part of me curious to know if he feels a certain type of way about her being in town, considering their history. It can't be something they just brush by surely. The other part of me would rather stay unknowing and uncaring towards anything bringing the two of them back together.

"Not sure, it'd be nice to see her again though." He shrugged.

A pang of jealousy shot through me, unbeknownst to why. If Theo wants to rekindle his spark with Olivia, what's stopping him? Definitely not me, I've made it pretty clear that I don't want a relationship with him. Well, not that I don't *want* it, more like I don't want to ruin our friendship. I can't lose him.

"You should take her to your restaurant. Successful people work amazingly together." I said through another big mouthful of food.

"Speaking of my restaurant," He slumped back in the sofa next to me, "I have some news." He was visibly trying to stop himself from smiling.

"Go on…" His almost smile was already spreading fully to mine.

"I talked to a couple businessmen last week, and they've been organising something which they finally got back to me about. Well, I-uh, I'm going to open up a new branch in New York." He looked at me, examining my face to look for somewhat of a response.

"What?!" My jaw dropped open, pride immediately surging through my body. I leant forward, slinging my arms around his neck and pulling him into a hug, "That's amazing, T. I'm so proud of you." I squealed right into his ear, "Are you going to go out there?" I pulled away from him, excitedly bobbing in my seat.

"The woman I'm signing my contract with said they're going to fly me out by the end of the week." His dimples poked through his cheeks as he broke eye contact with me, looking into his lap and playing with his hands.

"This is so exciting." I stood up pacing, unable to contain my excitement, "We have to pack you a suitcase, you have to call me every day and you have to tell me everything and, oh my god this is so exciting!" I paced back over to him, grabbing his hands and pulling him up and jumping into his arms, hugging him.

"You're more excited than I am." He laughed deeply, placing me back down on the floor after squeezing me in a hug for a couple seconds, "I'm going to miss you." He tucked a loose strand of hair behind my ear, his smile dissipating.

"How long will you be going for?" I took a breath, calming my excitement.

"Just 4 days, early Saturday to late Tuesday, so I'll see you on Wednesday." He placed a kiss on my forehead.

"I'll pick you up from the airport Tuesday night. *And* we'll just have to spend every waking moment together until you leave." I hugged him tightly.

"**S**orry I haven't called you sooner, I've been... busy." I held the phone to my ear whilst mixing my icing furiously.

"I know, not to make you feel self-conscious but the entire office knows about it. Carly and I have been trying to shut the rumours down but only so much you can do." Parker spoke through the phone, clearing his throat, "About the other night... the guy who was in your house?"

"I'm so sorry about that Lucas, my god, he's just a friend, I promise." I sighed.

"It's fine, I actually, I should apologise to you. I saw you talking with Brady and I got all...in your face- and I-"

"Woah, slow down, nothing is going on between Brady and I and nothing *ever* will." I scoffed that he thought anything could remotely happen when we're both completely sober.

There was a silence on his end of the line before he cleared his throat, "Can I call you back later? A-uh, friend is coming over." I could almost hear the blush rise on his face.

"Don't do anything that I wouldn't do, have fun." I laughed at him trying to conceal the fact that he has a girl over.

Something I love about Lucas Parker. No matter what has happened in the past between us, what happens when we're intoxicated or tensions are high, we will always be able to have a normal conversation, have a nice light-hearted joke or tell each-other about anything we're going through. Him and Carly are really what had gotten me through 4 years of moody Miles Brady, I would've gone insane, quicker than I have, without them.

I grabbed the tray out of the oven, placing it on the side

before the front door flew open, Theo walking in with 5 bags balancing in his arms.

I quickly untied my apron, dropping it on the counter and running over to him before taking half the shopping bags into my hands.

"You know I can do my own grocery shopping when you're gone? I'm not completely useless." I chuckled, ruffling through the paper bags and taking out the cupcake decorations I asked him to buy.

I threw a dollop of icing on each cupcake, slowly swirling it into a spiral with a spoon. Theo snuck up behind me grabbing a cupcake off the rack and taking an enormous bite before I could even stop him, "Hey! They aren't...done." I frowned, "No eating until they're fully frosted, T!" I smacked him on the chest, causing him to choke on the mouthful that he had spilling out of his mouth through his laughter and hysterical apologies.

"Well, we have to leave in 20 minutes so if you're going to be done by then, then I'll wait, but..." He took the one that I had just finished layering the icing onto, "I'll have to take another." He pressed the cupcake against my cheek, leaving a smudge of icing drooping down my cheek.

My jaw dropped open, as I grabbed a bag of flour, tossing a handful at him and ducking behind the counter, not at all trying to conceal my laugh.

He snuck round the other side of the kitchen island, picking me up effortlessly, startling me and causing me to drop the almost full bag of flour on the floor, making it explode *everywhere.*

He immediately put me down, both of us trying to stifle our giggles, "You're lucky you're leaving in a couple days otherwise I would be so mad at you right now." I giggled, shaking my head, "Make yourself useful and pack up the cupcakes, I have to clean up before we leave." I slung my jumper over the top of my head and threw it onto the kitchen counter, already looking a lot cleaner than I did a few seconds prior.

"Why is it so empty?" I strolled up the red staircase, almost tripping and losing my footing a few times.

"Because people are normal, and normal people don't watch horror movies in the cinema." I felt Theo throw a handful of popcorn at me from a few steps behind me.

I turned into the row we had booked our seats on, immediately regretting not bringing a different hoodie. There are actually no valid, excusable reasons why cinemas are so cold. No reason at all.

I settled in my seat; the movie starting and immediately jumpscaring us within the first 20 seconds. So, *this* is why we're the only people in this screen right now.

"You're shaking, are you scared?" Theo whispered, turning his attention away from the movie.

You know when horror movies get eerily quiet and you know you're about to get your heart blown into a million tiny pieces? That was the stage of the movie that we were at.

"Aside from the fact that I am waiting on being scared shitless, no, I'm just cold." I curled my legs into my chest and tucked my chin onto my knees in a ball shape.

"Here." Theo lifted his hoodie off of his body, his top rising slightly alongside it, using the other hand to hold the popcorn still in his lap.

My eyes couldn't help but glue themselves to his abs which poked through his shirt. I knew he went to the gym occasionally on his days off but *my God*.

"My eyes are up here, sweetheart." His voice resonated,

echoing through the empty walls, sending a chill through my spine.

My eyes snapped to make eye contact with him. He gave me a smirk, raising his eyebrows before handing me his hoodie and pulling his shirt back down. I quickly pulled it over my head, trying to conceal the blush that was flowing through my cheeks, the darkness not hiding it well enough.

By the time I managed to take a breath and pull the hoodie completely over my head, I noticed that Theo still had his glances set on me. He reached into my lap, grabbing a cupcake from the container that I was holding firmly in my grasp, unwrapped it and took a slow bite, all while making unforgiving eye contact with me.

"You're going to miss the movie if you keep looking at me." I cleared my throat, trying to sound less nervous than I was.

I was completely flushed with nerves, of course I had my moments but never had I ever felt so on edge, so full of tension around Theo of all people. I mean, it's made sense more recently than ever but at the same time that's Theo! That's my best friend, who's been there for me through thick and thin and who has loved me absolutely unconditionally from day 1.

"You're distracting me." I felt his voice shift closer to my ear.

"Now, who's fault is that?" I finally gave in, turning my head to face him, realising he was a lot closer than I anticipated.

His lips were moist, hung slightly apart. I could see his chest rising and falling at triple speed from 100 miles away, his eyes flicking between my own and my lips.

"You're the one dressed like the most beautiful person I have ever seen." His lip turned up, him biting it and resisting a full smile.

"I look like this every day. In fact, I look worse right now than I do on a normal day." I shook my head, turning to face away from him again, mainly to console the outrageous grin that was forming on my face right now.

"Well, it drives me absolutely insane every day." He whispered right next to my ear. He placed his hand gently on my chin, slowly turning me to face him again. He brushed the hood off of my head, his eyes frantic and scanning my every feature.

"Theo." I whispered, not being able to get much out of myself right now.

"Ellie?" He finally paused on my eyes, finally breaking into a smile, "Can I kiss you?"

All I can do is nod, instinctively, unassumingly, not even questioning what he just asked me, and without hesitation he pulled me towards him, holding my cheek as if it was the only thing keeping him centred, as if I was the rock keeping him at the bottom of the ocean, no matter how forgiving or merciful he became for air, we only dove deeper.

As unfamiliar as it was, our lips danced with one another, as if this is what we had been searching for our entire lives. The final moment in which fate and destiny alongside hopes and wishes had finally met, anchoring their hearts to one another and colliding in perfect harmony.

He kissed me again and again and again, not wanting to break apart, with the fear that perhaps he, we, would never encounter such bliss again. The hunger, the desire, the lust and need acquired for him all released in this moment. Released through me. Now I feel all these things, these emotions that I hadn't even had a second thought about in the past now has become my every waking thought that would not go long forgotten.

He pulled away, keeping his hand delicately rested on my cheeks, our foreheads pressed together, our breaths heaving in sync. Our smiles forming in sync.

"You have no idea how long I've wanted to do that." He shook his head against mine.

"I think I could make an accurate guess." I chuckled, the sound resonating through both us, him laughing too and reconnecting our kiss.

# Chapter Eight

I walked through the hall, waiting for Theo to bring the car around, into the bathroom and was hit with the most horrible, rotting scent ever. The entire place was eerily empty, employees only, empty. Not even that, there were 2 workers, looking at me like I wasn't supposed to be there. I almost asked them if I was doing something wrong, it was that eerie.

The smell really caught me off guard, I wanted to get out there just as quickly as I walked in and so I opened the door to the first stall to my right.

Oh my God. *Oh. My. God.*

The entire stall was drenched crimson red, dripping from the walls, the ceiling and eventually completely covering my peripheral and my entire body. I felt myself become paralysed to the spot, a body fading into my vision. It slowly rose from a sitting position to standing right in front of my face, eyes closed, but completely blacked out, floating but utterly limp but completely invading my personal space, but still leaving me unable to run. Unable to scream, shout, or release any form of emotion that I was currently feeling. Xs began forming onto the walls of the stall I was now sat in, in slashing movements, until my entire vision was scattered in Xs drawn in blood, footsteps leading me out the stall.

I finally regained the feeling of my feet, noticing the pain of paralysis easing throughout my body. I slowly stood up, like I was relearning how to walk all over again. Following the footsteps, placing my feet directly in the patches of emptiness amongst the bloody floor, led me directly to a door. A red door with no handles, whether it was red, painted or splashed that way, I don't know, but the feeling of fear was simply no longer a concern in my mind, as if unconsciously I pushed it open. Only for this nightmare to get a thousand times worse. There it was again, the figure, crouched in an all-black outfit, hood up, concealing its identity. In front of them was a girl, tied up, tape over her mouth with a look of utter pain in dismay amongst her expression. Her speech was muffled, but through the intense eye contact that pierced into my soul I felt like I was responsible for her misery. Yet all of a sudden, her voice screamed into my mind as if it was reality yelling right into my ear to save her.

"Save me! Please! Help me. Save me! Save me!"

"Save" the word echoed through my mind, rippling the one word into a thousand sounds. "Save."

"Save!"

"You're safe."

"You're safe."

"You're safe. It's okay."

"It's okay Els, you're safe." I felt an arm squeeze my shoulder, surging me back through what felt like an alternate dimension.

I jolted awake, choking on what felt like an entire gallon of water, trying to regain my breath from drowning in my own air.

Again, I was completely drenched in my own sweat, gasping as if it was either my very first, or bitter last breath in this world.

"Ellie, you're safe, it's just me. It's just Theo." He cradled me into his arms, my body not consciously responding to his grasp yet but my mind so scarily active to the point of terror. I could see every scream, every bloody murder, every victim flashing through my mind at 1000 miles an hour like a picture slideshow clicking through each memory as if there were a time frame for me to forget.

Regaining control of my body, yet still uncontrollably quivering, I managed to sit back up, running my fingers through and smoothing out my knotty hair.

"What's wrong? What happened? Why are you out here?" Theo tenderly kissed the top of my head, taking his side of the blanket and wrapping it around my shoulders.

No matter how consciously present I was, my mind was still adjusting to the horror which it had created itself; which is the worst thing about it. No matter how much torment, pain and horror I endure in the period of my dreams, my mind is the one responsible. I am the one responsible.

I took in my surroundings, realising I was asleep on the sofa, even though consciously remembering going to sleep, kissing Theo goodnight after our...date? If that's what you would call it.

"I- I. I don't know. It was like the feeling, the feeling of a vision but also it was just horrific. It was disgusting I-" I felt bile rising in my throat, a burning sensation that was never pleasant. I could still hear the squelching of the flesh and blood beneath my feet with every step I took. I heard him sigh at the mention of my visions again.

I quickly unravelled from the blanket and Theo's touch, rushing to the bathroom and heaving into the toilet, emptying every content in my stomach over the last 24 hours.

The subtle sound of footsteps echoed from behind me, Theo yawning but crouching next to me with a cool glass of water, which sent a chill up my spine to the touch.

"I'm sorry." I murmured, my head still half in the toilet bowl, "What time is it?"

"It's 4am, well, 3:59" He sat next to me rubbing my back.

My heart dropped at the familiar time. 3:59, this must be some kind of cruel universal joke. Something that I'd done to Mother nature and now she's playing some cruel trick on my mind.

I sulked back to my spot on the sofa, grabbing the glass of water on my way and flopped onto the chair. Finally feeling stable enough, I noticed my shoes and coat dropped to the floor, away from my coat rack and just... in the middle of the kitchen. Odd. Nothing to think much of, right? I barely remember coming in last night, I fell asleep in the car on the way home and straight away got into bed. Or, got on the sofa. I don't know.

"Honestly Ellie Bells, my life is *so* boring now. After I graduated, I did another degree in English. I jumped between podcasting and blogging then journalism then law for a little while, but I've moved back to London for law school." Olivia explained, with a beaming smile on her face.

"That's so cool, honestly, I'm envious." I held my hands up in surrender.

"Well... what about you? Tell me everything!" She reached

out and placed her hand on top of mine, covering the handle of my coffee mug.

"I mean, there's not much to update you on Olivia, I'm just taking every day in my stride." Not really knowing where I was going with my sentence, I continued, "I'm actually looking for another job right now, maybe even a little part time job at Theo's restaurant." I joked.

She choked as I finished my sentence, grabbing her napkin and dabbing her lip from the spilt coffee, "Theo's restaurant. He-did-it." She mumbled under her breath.

"What was that?" I didn't quite hear what she said since she mumbled while taking her sip from her abnormally large mug.

"I just remember him talking about it when we were younger, it was his biggest dream and he did it." She smiled, fiddling with her hands in her lap, "I can't believe he didn't say!" She shook her head dramatically.

"What do you mean he didn't say?" I asked, confused. Maybe Theo reached out to her, just like he said that he would.

"I bumped into him at the store yesterday. Guess we didn't get around to the career section of the conversation huh." She chuckled, her cheeks blushing pink, "How are you two? I'm assuming you keep in contact." She cleared her throat, rein-stating eye contact with me.

"We're good. We see each other basically every day." I laughed, more to clear the awkwardness than as a humour reaction. I didn't necessarily picture discussing Theo and I's rela-tionship with his ex-girlfriend who's just come back to town. For all I know she came back to London with the intention of rekindling their little flame and venging on me for having a part in their breakup.

"That's great, Ellie." She pressed her lips together, sucking her teeth together, and abruptly getting up, "I should get going,

I have a meeting in 20 minutes." She got her wallet out and placed a £50 note on the table.

We got *2 coffees.* It was like she was trying to rub it in my face how rich and successful she was.

"Keep the change, honey, see you soon!" She blew me a double kiss and strutted off, her pony tail doing its own walk behind her.

Just as she walked away, I felt myself glaring daggers into her back until the moment she was out of sight. I will never admit that I'm jealous but I'll admit I'm spiteful. How can someone, my age, be throwing £50 on the table like it's nothing. And the audacity to tell me to keep the change? Just as I thought I could make a new friend in this ugly world; the most condescending rich princess comes bouncing over to me giving me a fake grin. But I'll take it. Olivia Charlotte is not someone on my bucket list to be on the bad side of.

I held my head in my hands, about to call it a day and head home before a familiar face came beaming over to me, smiling as if she caught the last cookie in the shop.

"Hey *bebita!* What're you doing here?" Carly sat down in front of me with a million and one shopping bags piled around her, "I was just shopping for my birthday." She grinned, bouncing.

My heart skipped a beat, tricking me into thinking I missed her special day before reassuring myself it wasn't until next month, "I just had a coffee with a friend, you have a plan for the big day?" I smiled, trying to peer inside of her shopping bags.

"Nothing big, probably just a party, maybe 40 or 50 people, you know, the usual." The excitement radiated off her face like a kid in a candy store.

Nothing big, and then proceeding to say 40 or 50 people is something only Carly would correlate with one another.

"So, I bought this dress, and this skirt, this shirt too..."

Carly began pulling items of clothing out of her bags, showing me one by one as I slowly began to zone out on her, my mind occupied elsewhere. All that was on my mind was getting back home, asking Theo about Olivia and just completely clearing my mind.

"How come you didn't say you ran into Olivia yesterday?" I dumped my coat and bag onto the sofa and stomped off to where Theo was standing cooking in the kitchen.

He stopped fiddling about with whatever clutter he was doing and paused with his back towards me, "I didn't think it was necessary. Not really all that important." He turned his head over his shoulder and looked at me guiltily.

"Right. Well, that's nice." I nodded, clenching my teeth, giving him a thumbs up.

"Hey, there's nothing going on, I promise, it was a coincidence and we were just catching up. I know it was a bit weird that I didn't tell you, I'm sorry, I didn't think anything of it." He came up behind me, placing his arms round me and resting his head on top of mine.

"I mean it's fine, you don't owe me anything to tell me that," I mumbled, leaning slightly into his embrace.

"Are you...jealous?" He craned his neck so we were making eye contact, his mouth mockingly forming into a smile.

"What? No. No way. You can talk to Olivia Charlotte and her beautiful blonde hair whenever you want." I slapped his arm, now picking at my nails.

I was telling the truth, I wasn't jealous. It wasn't jealousy, it was just... wistfulness. Who am I kidding? That's exactly the same thing. Who am I convincing if not even myself that I'm jealous of what they had...have, will have again if I don't step in and shoot my shot. This should be what I want. I'm done convincing and persuading myself I need something more or I should have something less.

"Well then, we should all go out sometime. Like old times."

Old times? You mean when you two used to date and you would desperately try to leave me out to prove you could be in a relationship with her and lose your feelings for me but it ended up not being true so you dumped her for me, leaving her to hate me because I didn't even have feelings for you at the time so you doomed your relationship for absolutely no reason?

"Sure." Is what I actually said, rolling my eyes.

"Come on, let's watch a movie. Last one before I have to leave." He nudged my shoulder, smiling sympathetically at me.

I immediately felt a surge of guilt, calling him out so quickly and harshly.

"Your pick." I bounced over to the sofa, throwing him the remote and settling down with one another.

## Chapter Nine

ELLIE

"I miss you. So, so much. I can't wait to come home to some cookies." He glitched slightly in between words.

I aimlessly wandered around, trying to find the best spot for signal in my house to make our FaceTime possible.

"I miss you too. How was your meeting?" I settled on the stool tucked into my kitchen island.

"It was amazing, we settled the big details, I'll explain better when I get home tomorrow."

"Amazing, I'll be right outside waiting." I promised, smiling at the sound of his croaky laugh down the phone.

With the time we've been apart, we haven't been talking as much, considering the time zone difference and the distance. Whenever I'm free, he's in a meeting, not that I'm ever *not* free or something but it seems like he is always busy. Success, yet again, touchy subject. I couldn't help my feet from swinging and a smile permanently pressed on my face when I first heard him pick up the phone. I knew this would be a good idea, I'm happy. I'm finally in a good place in my life and that is undoubtedly because of Theo.

We haven't talked about our kiss, but we also don't feel the need to. It felt right, it felt natural. It felt like I was a teenage girl all over again, staring at the new guy across the classroom, thinking about all the cute romantic possibilities that would happen if I were to just go over and talk to him. Except this time, I did talk to him, and this time he was my best friend.

"I'll call you before my flight, okay?" he blew me a kiss through the screen before waving sadly and hanging up the phone.

Today was a productive day, ever since Theo left, all I've been doing in sympathy baking and hopelessly looking at the stars all night, the thought that he could possibly be looking at the same ones, just elsewhere, giving me some sort of comfort. I haven't even been able to get much sleep at all. Whether that was because of Theo or just my internal fear of having another vision was a different story.

First mission was to stop by the office. Carly told me I forgot my endless supply of mugs, *what a shame,* and there's someone new moving into my desk next week so I need to come and pick them up.

Second mission is to pick up my car from the garage. Once Theo gets back, I won't be able to drive his anymore.

Third mission is to bake? Because absolutely why not.

"Hi *mi amorcito*!" Carly immediately sprung out of her seat once I entered the office, attracting attention and a few waves from my old co-workers.

"Hey Carly." I walked round her desk, sitting in the spare seat and began to swivel nervously.

"Here, I packed them up for you." She heaved a box from the underside of her desk, struggling to pull it properly. It's concerning how heavy it was considering I had only had 4 birthdays in the office, but no matter the occasion it was a 'have a mug, congratulations!' scenario.

I noticed Brady on the phone in his office as I swivelled round trying to help Carly with the ridiculous load, "I'll be right back." I untucked my seat, strutting over towards his office before I could change my mind about it.

I approached the door, knocking weakly, not wanting to distract him from his call too much. He looked between his laptop screen and me a couple times before finally speaking out, "Look. This can wait, right? Okay...Okay. Bye." He hung up, facing and paying all his attention to me.

"Good morning, Miss Easton." He leant back in his chair slightly, exposing more of his figure.

"Good morning, Mr. Brady." My cheeks flushed, "Can I...?" I gestured to the seat on the other side of his desk.

"Of course, take a seat." He nodded. I closed the door behind me, settling myself in front of his tough gaze.

"Do you need to report something?" He sat forward, placing his hands in a fist in front of mine.

"No. No, I-uh," truthfully, I had no clue why I was here. Sitting here, watching him stare me down. Part of me wanted to confide in him about my visions, from the minimal sympathy and help he showed me the last time that I was here. The other part of me was screaming that that was a bad idea. Right? Surely, it's fine.

"I know this is going to sound ridiculous but I had another vision." His expression dropped even further than I thought possible at my words, "It was at the cinema, off of the A51. It was...gruesome. It was horrible." I felt myself gag at the thought of recalling anything that happened, or that will happen.

"You need to call me if this happens again." He cleared his throat, finally breaking eye contact with me. He shuffled through his drawers, taking out a small piece of paper and scribbling something on it.

"This is my personal cell. I can't risk Prescott finding out about this or anyone, for that matter. That's my number and this is my address. Please use it if you need something. I'm being dead serious Easton." His hand rested on the paper, hovering in front of me, "Just in case, okay?"

I had no words. I nodded, taking the paper from his grasp and nodding slowly.

The door flung open before I could utter another movement or word, Prescott stood frantic at the door, a shocked expression on his face.

"Brady, on the road in 10, incident off of A51."

My heart dropped at his words, the first reaction I had since sitting in this chair. It felt like my heart was trying to combust out of my chest, my throat tightening to the point of no return. Brady glanced frantically between Prescott and I, eventually nodding and grabbing his ready back and walking out the door.

"Ellie." Prescott smiled in my direction before following Brady out of the room.

My feet were solidified against the floor, completely glued. I felt my body swaying, my stomach churning, I could've fainted, thrown up, passed out right then and there if it wasn't for my fight or flight reaction finally kicking in. I shot up, making a bee line for the exit. Why is it that almost every time I've been in this damn office, I have to make a run for my air before time decides I'm going to pass out?

I heard Carly calling my name in a panic of concern, witnessing complete déjà vu.

I was almost at the car before a tall, muscular figure completely stopped me in my tracks, pushing the air straight into my lungs and forcing me to take a breath.

"Easton, breathe." A hand brushed against my shoulder.

My vision focused on Brady's face, my lungs immediately listening to his voice, "Breathe."

I noticed him holding my box of mugs in one of his hands, effortlessly balanced in between his arm and his hip, his other hand still resting on my shoulder. I nodded, making pleading eye contact with him. I wanted to scream for his help, for him to hug me and tell me everything's okay. He believes me and he helps me. He wants to help me.

"I was just bringing this to your car." He pointed to the box that I couldn't even drag on the floor, "Miss Montana said it was the last of your desk things."

"Yeah, that's what I originally came here for." I finally managed to spit out something.

I walked over to my car, him pacing closely behind me in silence, packing the box into my boot and just standing in silence.

"Thank you for–"

"You should–"

We spoke at the same time, chuckling after.

"You first." He gave me a small smile.

"Thank you for the box. I mean, bringing it... to my car, and your number too." I tried to avoid eye contact with him, feeling his eyes on me either way.

"Of course."

"Now you." I smiled back.

"You should use it. My number." He looked down towards his feet. Seemingly nervous.

I simply nodded, receiving a nod back, a mutual end of conversation.

I watched him walk back towards Prescott, getting into the staff car. I stood for a second allowing the cold air to flood and refresh me, bringing my breathing and temperature back down to normal before Carly came rushing over.

"What did Brady say to you? Do I need to kill him?" She stormed over with Parker chasing her trail.

"Carly." I tried to calm her down before she escalated into her anger properly.

"Baby, I swear to God." She stopped directly in front of me, rubbing her hands together, her tongue tucked into her cheek.

"Carly. It's fine." I laughed quietly.

"No, because if he hurt your feelings...Ooo boy, *lo mataré*." She shook her head furiously. You know when Carly breaks out into Spanish, she means violence.

"Carly." Parker spoke up.

"Lucas Parker. If you say a word to defend that *brujo*." She warned him, her index finger sticking up.

He showed his hands in surrender, shooting me a scared expression.

"Carly, he actually helped me. Don't kill him." I brought her into a hug and nuzzled my face into her shoulder, giving Parker a thumbs up behind her back.

"Okay." She took a deep breath, "Hold on. Brady's helping you? He must be head over heels." She slapped me on the arm, giggling and turning to face Parker. His face flushed and he shot me a nervous look.

"I've got to get going, they're waiting for me, it was nice seeing you again, Ellie." He smiled before jogging over to the staff car which was still parked near the car park exit.

"Am I crazy or is he completely wrapped around your little finger?" I nudged her.

"Puh-lease. Lucas? No way." She rolled her eyes, looking over her shoulder to Parker who'd just walked back into the building.

"Sure." I laughed, "Look, I have to go pick up my car but I'll call you later." I kissed her on the cheek, waving goodbye and getting into my car.

# Chapter Ten

## MILES

"You have 10 seconds to explain what the fuck is going on and how she knows, before I walk out there myself and arrest her." Prescott slammed his hands against the wall, his audience jumping in shock.

"Again." One of the guys from the Michigan state team cleared his throat, avoiding eye contact with me.

"Look, I don't have a clue what is going on with her, all I know is that she's handy to have around." I shrugged, trying to downplay how much I *know* we were both relying on each other at the moment.

I stood, staring at the blood bath, exactly how she described it. Gruesome...horrible.

"We need to look for evidence." Prescott handed us all a pair of blue rubber gloves, designating us our areas to search for clues.

I have no clue where this was all going, with these crimes, with Easton, with Prescott or this new team we've gotten in to help us out but I've got a bad feeling about all of this. Maybe I should just leave her alone, maybe none of this would happen if

I didn't get involved with her. That's impossible. A ridiculously stupid idea. Not only can I just not do that, but it would be wrong in a million ways. She's relying on me to help her and that's exactly what I need to do.

"If she comes to you for help again, you know what to do hm?" Prescott nodded towards me.

I stayed completely silent, not wanting to agree to the absurdity Prescott was expecting from me.

"Otherwise, your job is on the line." He mumbled, walking in the opposite direction.

I rolled my eyes, pulling on my rubber gloves, allowing my thoughts of Easton to breeze through my mind, distracting me from the criminality I had to poke and prod through. It helped. The thought of her helped and that terrifies me, through and through. I can't let it get too deep

# *Chapter Eleven*

## ELLIE

" It's lovely to see you again, Ellie." Dr. Taylor smiled at me from across the room as I got settled on the sofa directly across from her, "How's everything been since our last session?"

"As good as it can be, I guess." I shrugged, forcing a fake smile onto my face.

"How are you feeling about the aftermath or the vision? Have you talked to Theo about boundaries and what makes you comfortable or uncomfortable? Whenever you're ready." She prompted me to continue.

I took a deep breath, trying desperately to swallow the knot that was tightening in my throat before proceeding, "Actually, I've actually uh- I've had another vision since I last saw you, and I think it came true again." I swallowed, not making eye contact with her so I couldn't decipher her probably judgmental expression.

"And what was it about this time?" She pushed.

I blinked away the tears forming in my eyes, not wanting to tell her that she might as well diagnose me a psychopath in this very given moment, "It was about a crime again. Not at all legal. At all." I choked on my own words, starting to feel sick at the thought.

Brady knows that it's happened again, coincidentally in that moment he was called to the crime scene, which was obviously just my luck.

"And do you think that you were somehow subconsciously involved with the crime?" Her eyebrows creased in worry.

"Yes. No. I mean no. There's no way I could've been but I feel *so* guilty."

She closed her notebook, shuffling her chair closer towards me, "The thing about guilt is that our brain," She puts her hands up, motioning around her head, "We have built in defence mechanisms which protect us from the real guilt that we would experience from something that we really want, no matter how awful those desires are. It's all about our hidden intuition. We... You can't control that. And as scary as it can be, as unwilling you are to respond to that, you should perhaps consider yourself lucky that that's all they are, just visions." She pressed her lips into a line, shrugging and shuffling back again.

I had no response to anything she just said. What I heard was, 'you're crazy, and your brain is trying to stop you from murdering someone.'

I took a breath, trying to get the words out of my mouth to acknowledge what she was saying.

It seems as though she understood and continued to change the subject, "Shall we move on to talk about the relationships in your life? Perhaps Theo, or anyone else who can support you during this time?" She tilted her head.

I finally mustered up the courage to start talking again, "There's Carly. She's my best friend from work. She doesn't know, but we just... have fun together, I guess. There's also, uh, Brady?" I questioned myself, unbelieving that I would consider him someone I would be able to go to for support, "Brady's my boss. My ex-boss. I went to the office to pick up some of my things and he actually told me to call him...if I need him." I reflect on how ridiculous I sound in comparison to how much I hated him the last time I saw Dr. Taylor. I mean, I never even hated the guy. He hated me, which is the confusing thing about all of this, because apparently, he never did. He's just *a very private person, Miss Easton.*

"So, would you say you trust Brady? You would seek safety in him?"

"That's a bit far, all he's been is a piece of shit to me for 4 years so I don't know why all of a sudden he's on my side." Brady's on my side. The word's echoed through my mind, the more times I think about it, the more absurd it sounds, "Who knows what's going to happen." I groaned, holding my head in my hands.

"It will sort itself out, Brady isn't someone you should worry about. Trust and believe in yourself and it'll work out okay in the end." She smiled cheerily.

"If I'm being completely honest with you Dr. Taylor, I'm just scared. I don't know what I'm capable of if I'm waking up in random places, not remembering the night before and I'm scared. What if something is wrong with me? What if I'm hurting people?" I broke my shield, letting one, then another and another tear slip, quickly wiping my eyes before I could let my guard down anymore.

"Your fear and your strength outweigh each other. Allow yourself to have courage and bring yourself through it."

"Theo!" I ran up to him, jumping into his arms and wrapping my legs around his waist.

He held me with his spare hand and hugged me back, nuzzling his face into my neck and placing a quick kiss onto my lips and placing me down.

"Oh Els, I missed you so much." He grabbed my face with both his hands and shook his head slightly, "It's like a fever dream, felt like I wouldn't be back for forever." He tenderly kissed my forehead, staying there for a few seconds and then pulling away.

I pulled him eagerly to the car, getting in and immediately driving off, almost not giving him enough time to actually get in. The excitement of seeing him again had the adrenaline pumping through my body at a million miles per hour. Just that feeling of comfort and familiarity in a person that you feel so at home and natural with.

"Tell me all about it." I still had a smile planted on my face.

"Right, so I signed the contract and the lease for the building, basically giving them the go ahead to start refurbishing and actually making it look presentable. They said they'll need me back there soon to approve planning amongst other things, but all in all, very successful." He explained, his smile also beaming.

"I'm so proud of you. This is insane. Unbelievable." I stuttered, unable to comprehend that *my* Theo is an international restaurant owner. In New York!

"Couldn't have done it without my number one supporter." He rested his hand on my thigh sending a jolt of electricity up my body.

I smiled weakly; my brain unable to distract itself from the circles his thumb was making.

"I actually got you something. I immediately just thought of you when I saw it, I had to." My heart uncontrollably fluttered at his words. The absolute bare minimum but such a cute, wholesome thought.

I pulled up to the traffic lights, turning to face him ruffling through his bag.

"Here." He pulled out a snow globe, with Lady Liberty in the centre, the top of the globe scattered with different constellations.

"Oh my God." I took it from his grasp, shaking it, "It's beautiful, I love it. Thank you." I grinned, glancing between him and the snow globe.

A loud honk distracted me from my gift, realising the light was green and quickly adjusting myself to start driving again. I bit my lip to try and contain my smile but obviously failing. It's like a chore; a competition or a challenge not to smile around him, it's just absolutely impossible and I fail every time.

⁓

"Do you know when you have to go back?" I mumbled through a mouthful of chocolate chip, freshly baked as promised to Theo.

"Mm, within the next 2 weeks, they didn't actually want me to leave but I *obviously* had to come home. Important reasons." He spoke through a mouthful of cookie.

"Oh, yeah? What important reasons?" I chuckled, throwing my legs over his lap.

"These cookies are number 1 for sure." He picked up another from the cooling rack while putting the rest of his 4th into his mouth.

I laugh and shake my head, "These cookies would be absolutely nothing without their baker, you know." I hit him gently on the arm.

"*I* would be nothing without their baker." He leant into me, resting his head on my chest.

No doubt he could hear my heart beating like a thousand drums. I adjusted my arm so it was hung over his shoulder and he shuffled into me, now completely laying in between my legs. I moved my free hand into his hair, gently tracing his faint, wild curls.

"I'm going to miss you when you go." I whispered, not meaning to actually say it out loud.

"Come with me." He flipped himself over in my lap, now staring up at me with those beautiful brown doe eyes.

"Don't be silly, I can't." I shook my head, breaking eye contact with him and flopping my head back onto the arm rest.

He stayed quiet for a minute, rolling off of me and standing up, "I should get going." He cleared his throat.

I shot up, standing next to him, him still towering over me, "I thought you were going to stay with me tonight?" I sulked, giving him puppy dog eyes and knowing he can't say no to that.

He looked away, with a faint smile on his face, "Yeah, I know, I'm just exhausted and need to sort a few things out early tomorrow. Don't want to wake you." He pulled me into his grasp, resting his chin on the top of my head.

"Fine. I'll see you tomorrow anyway?" My voice muffled into his chest.

"Of course." He placed a kiss on the top of my head, not quite letting go of our hug yet.

This was nice. It was warm. A feeling of security and ease enveloped and wrapped into the arms of home. I could stay with him all day. He is where I feel safest, happiest, most myself. He makes my own home warmer than it is simply by stepping in the front door with his beaming smile and precious gaze. When he holds me it's like everything else in the world melts away and it's just me in his grasp. I've always loved hugs from

Theo, whether I felt the way I did a month ago...or whether I feel the way I do now. The real question is what has changed? What moment altered my brain chemistry to see him in the new light that I do? The romantic gestures have always been sweet, but that's all they were... sweet. They were cute, they were nice, they were simple. But they *are* mine. They *are* ours, and nothing in this world has ever come between Theo and I, and in this very given moment, physically, nothing could either.

He pulled away from my hug, placing one last kiss on my forehead, a cold breeze suddenly chilling me as he picked up his coat and bag, said goodbye and headed out the front door.

I flopped back down on the sofa, taking a deep breath. Knowing I have a lot to decide, a lot to think about, a lot to talk about with him. As much as we could carry on as it is and it be absolutely perfect; it's bound to get confusing and simply misleading for the both of us, and the last thing that I want to do is hurt him.

# Chapter Twelve

## ELLIE

Screaming, *begging* 'Help me please. Mercy. Mercy. MERCY. MERCY. M E R C Y.' A flash of an unfamiliar place faded through my vision; it was dark. Eerie. Misty. Just like the alleyway, but it felt different. I could feel the difference in the air on my skin, it was thick and dusty. The smog filled my lungs and I could feel my heart slowing in my chest. Or was it speeding up? My chest was tight, almost impossible to move and breathe in the endless darkness. I couldn't see him. He needs my help and I can't see him. The muffled screams choked as if it was smothered by something, silenced or restricted. My legs finally began striding hurriedly, as if I wasn't in control of my own pace or my own body, just the awareness that I could finally move. The splashes of the puddles erupting under my feet, the drops of rain hitting against me, getting more and more frequent with every step I took. I'm drenched. Searching for the voice. *His* voice, but nothing.

Silence.

Breathing. His breaths were slow, shallow, very faint. Intertwined with my quick, sharp exhales and the force of gravity dragging me through the floor, throwing me in circles until I was finally thrown back into reality screaming.

Almost instinctively, I grabbed my phone, pressing Theo's number, without even consoling my breaths at first, desperate to hear his calm tone. The only tone that sounded was the dial tone. Over, and over again. It was morning. The glare of the sun through the window blinded me, and alongside the panic, and sheer fear that I felt enveloping me second by second didn't help. My heart beat rose to my throat, a sick feeling drowning me as well as memory of the boy in my dream.

The next registered number below Theo's was Brady. His words echoed through my mind, *'Please use it if you need something. I'm being dead serious, Easton.'* So that's exactly what I do.

"Get inside, you'll catch a cold." He pulled me out of the rain by my shoulder, rubbing my shoulders to warm me up, "Let me grab you a jumper." He retreated off down the hallway.

I stood awkwardly by the front door, not wanting to overstep any more than I already have. A month ago, if someone would have told me I'd be standing in Miles Brady's house, soaked by the rain and waiting for him to get me a jumper, I would have laughed in their face.

"Please ignore the state of me, it's been a bit of a hectic morning... and the state of the house too." He ran his hand through his hair, looking around and taking a deep breath out and handing me a black hoodie that had a strong woody, earthy scent.

"It's okay, don't worry about it." I took a few steps in,

taking off my wet hoodie and pulling his over my head, admiring the warmth and comforting vibe of his home. It was the right amount of modern and modest to make a house a home.

Just as he was about to speak a loud clatter and the sound of running footsteps came hurling towards us, "Daddy, Daddy! I found it! I found the red paint!" A little girl with the longest brown hair I've ever seen on a child came jumping out from down the corridor, with different assortments of paint colours splattered all over her arms and dress. The second that she noticed me, her arms dropped to her side, hiding the red tin behind her.

"That's great sweetheart, go and finish your painting, I'll come and see it when you're finished." He crouched down in front of her, her little body completely hidden behind him.

She poked her head round the side of him, looking directly at me, "Who's that Daddy? She's very pretty. She looks a bit like-"

"Okay Mae, off you go."

She tottered off down the hallway before Brady turned back to face me, sighing and looking at me nervously.

"Mae?" I smiled, warmed by the wholesome interaction I had just witnessed.

"Yeah, I-uh, well, Maeve." He stuttered, making many hand gestures trying to explain.

"She's adorable, Brady." I nodded to him, breaking eye contact with him and walking towards the sofa, sitting down and taking in my surroundings. Taking in my first out of work interaction with Miles Brady and his daughter. That's definitely not something I thought I would ever hear myself say. It makes me wonder about what other secrets he has in his life. *Nobody* knows the real him in the office and this proves it. If he has a wife or girlfriend...whoever Maeve's mum is...

"How're you feeling? Do you want a drink? Maybe some food?" He hovered next to me, not sitting yet and playing with his hands.

"I'm fine, Brady, let's just... talk." I shrugged, not really knowing where to go with this. It felt foreign actually having someone willing to sit down and talk to me about what I was feeling, thinking...seeing. Someone that I wasn't paying to listen to me talk about my life and ask me questions I don't know answers to. He just genuinely wants to help me.

"It felt so much more like a dream this time. I couldn't see much, I couldn't make anything out, only this boy was yelling for mercy. There was a lot of water too and it felt like the air was thick, I couldn't breathe." I felt something resurfacing within me, the panic, the tightness, and almost immediately as it washed over me, and of course noticed, placing a hand on my shoulder.

"Just take some deep breaths. You're fine." He guided me, taking a deep breath with me multiple times, "Take it easy."

His voice eased its way into my soul, calming me, soothing me as if there were nothing to ever worry about in the first place. After taking our breaths, he gave me a sympathetic yet pitiful look, "Is there anything else you remember?" he twiddled his thumbs in circles, deep in concentration.

I shook my head, "Just loads of water. And rain." I shrugged, knowing that that tiny piece of information wouldn't be any more helpful than me being spooked by a dream.

He sighed deeply, pinching his bottom lip in between his fingers, "I don't know what to do here, Easton, this is confusing...it's..."

"Weird, crazy, I feel like I'm insane. There's no real, sane, logical explanation for this, right?"

"You aren't crazy. You're not insane, we'll figure this out."

He sat back against the arm rest and rubbed his face in his hands and over his hair.

"We?" I was confused at how much he's changed. Not only was he the last person I would think about talking to for anything but now I'm sitting in his front room, listening to him telling me that he's going to stick by my side and figure out my problems with me?

"Easton, I know I haven't been the nicest person to you, and I'm sorry. There's a reason behind my madness and I promise you that it's me, it has nothing to do with you because you're hard working and you're amazing... at what you do, and I would take you back in a heartbeat, to the team, if it was my decision." He stumbled over his words, sending red, green and amber signals flying across the room.

I paused for a second, really not knowing how to take this in. Knowing he values and appreciates me as much as he's implying and after all these years of hatred and bitterness, it's all been fake?

I felt a chill draft over me, my whole body erupting a shake.

"I'll put the fire on." He got up, kneeling in front of his fireplace and starting to fiddle with it.

A comfortable silence aired in the room, the rain still tapping against the window.

"Your house is beautiful, it's so cosy." I nestled myself further into his sofa.

"Thank you." He cleared his throat, still trying to light the fire.

"Let me help you." I got up, sitting cross-legged next to him, taking the matches from his hand, our fingers brushing one another slightly.

He gave me the match box, walking out of my peripheral before I felt a thick, warm blanket close over my shoulders as he sat back down next to me, glancing occasionally to make sure I was okay.

I watched as the fire grew, mesmerised by the colours and the movements of every flame, unable to tear my eyes from the colours.

# Chapter Thirteen

## MILES

How can someone be so peaceful whilst somehow on fire and burning the world around them? I can't tear my eyes from her. She can probably feel me staring at her but there's something so mesmerising about someone who just doesn't know how mesmerising they are. The way she's cuddled into *my* blanket, in *my* jumper, in front of *my* fireplace and I can't tear *my* eyes away from *her*. I could see the fire blazing in the reflection of her eyes, giving them a newfound light that isn't usually perceived when you first see her but when she's distracted, throwing her head back when she laughs, slapping the arm of whoever she's laughing with, that's when the glimmer slips out, and you've got to be careful because as quickly as it beams, is as quickly as it dims. How many times have I watched her, heard her laugh across the room and wanted to go over there and laugh with her. But I couldn't, I shouldn't have but after 4 years could you forgive a man for giving in? I just wanted to save her from my baggage, and now I know her baggage, I don't think I'll forgive myself for placing mine on her too.

I pulled my vision off of her, feeling my face flush...because of the heat from the fire of course. The warmth escaped from the fireplace, hugging me. This familiarity, comfort, this warmth was so foreign, so forgotten, yet so homely. But the fire, the blankets and the jumpers can only bring so much warmth. Ellie sitting by my side, feeling like the warmest hug I could possibly get, feeling like home. But I shouldn't say that.

How does one move past grief if grief is in every corner of his own home? If Ellie is sitting where *she* used to be, in *my* home, with *my* daughter in the next room over. Just like how it used to be and never will be again. Guilt and grief hand in hand may be worse than lonesome grief itself. Grief is love's last love letter, its receipt, its memoir, if you will. You take too long to cherish it and it's ripped away from you faster than you can acknowledge what it is. I can't have another goodbye from love again.

*'Love her like you love me. Move on Miles, for Maeve if not for yourself.'* 7 years and I've failed her words to me. She gave me her blessing yet my heart was ripped out, laid in her hand and left in that very room that we entered together but she never left. Never to be given to another. But with Ellie, the faint beating in my chest resurfaces, it aches, it's sickening. But of all the people I would choose to let into my *life,* my *daughter's life,* and my *past?* It would be her, her and her fire eyes.

"Are you okay?" Her small voice snapped me out of my never-ending stream of thoughts. Her gaze now focused on me, a small smile taunting her lips.

"Of course, are *you* okay? Are you warm?" I pulled the blanket further on her shoulder, brushing her arm in the process. The slightest touch sending a thousand volts into my arm, a hopeful reaction to a hopeless possibility.

She opened her mouth to respond, letting her smile free, before being cut off by a harsh ringtone echoing from the other side of the room. She stood up, letting the blanket drop to the floor and picked up her phone.

"I'm sorry I called you so early, I just- I, uh, I thought you'd be up since...well yeah, I know now...no...no...but you said you would be up so that's why I called...okay...yep, sorry. No, I'll see you later...no not right now..." She glanced over to me, "I'll be home soon, but Theo I-... okay, sure...no 2 hours is fine... alright...bye bye." She dropped her phone back on the sofa, retreating back over to me and re-wrapping herself in the blanket.

"What did he want?" I cleared my throat, focusing on the fire.

"Nothing, I called him this morning, uh- before you, but he didn't answer. He was in a meeting, he did say that yesterday that he would be busy with work from early, I just forgot and he- yeah." She mumbled out, tears pooling in her eyes, returning her gaze to the flames.

"Well." I cleared my throat, not really knowing if I was overstepping but deciding to, anyway, "If it makes matters better? I'm glad you called. I'm glad you're here."

A small smile flickered on and off of her face, the warm glow of the fire making her face light up even more.

"I'm glad I'm here too." She eventually muttered out, as if she was trying to convince herself it was the right thing to say. She cleared her throat, shuffling herself out of the blankets hold and stood up, "Food?" She beamed, looking down at me hopefully, expectantly.

"Food." I nodded, jumping up.

I called Maeve to come help us, no doubt she would get upset with me if she found out that I cooked without her. Not that she's any help at all, but according to her, sitting on the counter and tasting every time I add a new ingredient counts as 'cheffy stuff'.

Seeing Ellie and Maeve interact was something that I didn't know was missing from my life. Something I didn't know I needed. Weirdly, it felt like closure, closure that I didn't know would find me so soon. Closure that I didn't think I was ready for. Clearly, I'm way ahead of my time, maybe even in over my head.

Their smiles and sounds of their giggles merging together, Ellie cradling Mae's head in her arms whenever she does something a little too cute or Mae insisting on Ellie cooking the rest of lunch with her on her back. It all felt too familiar and part of me wanted to shove it in the other direction and never look back, but part of me loved this for Maeve, it really did seem like a good thing for her. I just don't want her to get too attached to Ellie. For reasons. As bad as that sounds, as much as I would love to keep Ellie around, with her visions, and my job and her complicated situationship with Theo, it's just, incompatible. Impossible. Inconvenient.

# *Chapter Fourteen*

## ELLIE

"No. Stop fighting me. I'm at your service today, you get to stay in bed." Theo insisted, tucking the blanket underneath me like a burrito.

"Theo, please, I'm suffocating." I choked out, my voice all croaky. When Brady told me *Get inside, you'll catch a cold,* I didn't realise that was him manifesting it for me to actually get sick.

Theo has had me in bed from the second I woke up this morning still with the shivers, *still in Brady's hoodie,* blanket on, blanket off, blanket on, blanket off, bringing me tea, soup, more tea, more soup. It was quite cute to be honest. He's taken the day off even though I insisted that he shouldn't and that I'd be okay. Good thing that he did because my legs are currently completely inoperable. Definitely because of the blanket burrito, not because I'm lazy.

He retreated back over to me, with another bowl of soup, "I'm so full, that better not be more soup." I groaned, burying my face into my pillow.

"I made a huge pot so you should just eat it." He placed it

on my bedside, taking the pillow from me and brushing the sweaty hairs stuck to my forehead, "You're burning up. Here." He placed a cold flannel on my forehead, sending a shiver through me.

"Thanks." I mumbled, looking up at his concerned, sympathetic expression, "I'm-"

"Don't you dare apologise to me Els." He leant down and placed a gentle kiss on my cheek, "I care *about* you, so I care *for* you." He kissed my other cheek.

He cares about me; he always has and he always will.

I sat up, bringing my face closer to his then I realised it would be.

"This is gonna sound absurd and crazy and completely out of the blue but you should just listen to me, alright?" I completely faced his direction, our faces mere inches apart.

"Trust me I've heard the fair share of absurdity from you Els." He chuckled, brushing a loose strand of hair out of my face.

I took a deep breath, preparing to let every one of my thoughts out to him.

"Throughout our entire friendship, you have always been everything that I've had, always and the truth is T, I've been so scared to lose that, that I've never even considered the fact that we could be something more. And that's all I've been able to think about since the cinema and I've never thought about it before then because I was scared, and I'm sorry that it's taken me so long to realise but...I'm not scared anymore. It's me and you T. It always has been." I sighed, running my fingers up his arm.

I never thought about it because I was scared, half-truth. I never thought about it because I never wanted that in particular? Maybe I was trying to convince myself that Theo was right for me. Pretending that this whole vision thing, being fired and all the downfalls happening in my life is the universe telling me to get a grip and hold on to what, or who, has been in front of me this entire time. This was me listening to the universe, taking matters into my own hands rather than leaving it up to the fate of the world. Since the world's favourite hobby is biting me in the ass right now, I figured it's time to turn around and bite it back. If I'm in control of everything and everyone that comes into my life then I can manipulate how my life is going to go. And being with Theo is exactly the step in the right direction that my mind needs. Needs turn into wants and vice versa. Whether they're forced or not.

Theo's eyes darted in between mine; he was biting the inside of his lip to stop his usual contagious grin from forming but the corners of his lips turned up nonetheless forcing his dimples to poke into his cheeks.

"You really mean it?" He leant forward, placing his hand on mine.

I nodded, taking a moment to consider what I was about to dive head first into. I know Theo better than anyone else, and he knows me like the back of his hand. He's been the only person who's been with me through every single stage of my life, right from the beginning. With everything that happened between him and Olivia he *still* made sure I was okay. I was always his priority. Everything that happened with my parents, and everything after that, right up until today. I'm done taking that for granted.

He cleared his throat, breaking eye contact for no longer than a second, before placing a gentle kiss on my cheek, lingering for a few seconds before pulling away.

"You forget that I know you better than anyone else in this world. My feelings for you will never change Els, I know you're in a... how do I say this nicely? A fragile place right now and I don't want to take advantage of that. I don't want to take advantage of having you." He cupped my cheek in his hand, studying my face deeply.

"I want this Theo, I promise. I'm not going to suddenly break down if we do this." I placed my hands on his shoulders, rubbing them up and down his neck.

He paused, sighing and nodded, like he was trying to convince himself this was a good idea. This was what he wanted, he's wanted this for 20 years and he's the one hesitating? The more he stutters about this, the more time I have to think about how bad of an idea this could actually be.

"You're right. You're completely right, sorry. I just... I want this to work." He brought his hands back to my face bringing our foreheads together and taking a deep breath, before extending his grasp around me and pulling me into a deep hug. Returning the hug, I could immediately feel his heart pounding in rhythm with mine.

"I do too." We pulled out of the hug, admiring each other in a new light for a second, "Can we go on a walk or something? I need to get some fresh air. I'll wrap up warm I promise." I smiled pleadingly, clasping my hands together and begging him.

"Sure. It's 27 degrees out though." He stood up, pulling the blanket back so I could shuffle out of bed.

"What? It was literally pouring down with rain yesterday?" I stopped in my tracks, confused.

"Apparently we're expecting a heatwave from today to next week." He shrugged, helping me up off the bed.

"Convenient." I took off Brady's hoodie, throwing it to the other side of my bed, standing in just my underwear for a second before pulling on some clean fresh clothes, spraying myself quickly with deodorant and body spray, giving myself a sniff, "On second thought, I'm gonna shower. I'll be right back."

## Chapter Fifteen

### THEO

"Okay, what about them?" She giggled, secretly pointing to the man, woman and 2 kids playing about 50 feet away from us.

"They're going through a rough patch, trying to stay together for the kids. She's way more detached than he is and has Tinder already reinstalled on her phone." I spat out as she gasped dramatically.

"He's completely clueless! He actually thinks he still has a chance after he cheated on her with her boss." She rolled her eyes, slapping my arm.

We both stayed quiet for a second, watching the family interact for a few more seconds before erupting into a fit of laughter. Whenever Els and I want to get out of the house with absolutely no intention of doing anything, we come to this exact spot and just people watch. It's our favourite pastime. The stories we've come up with are quite the story. Example, 2 men walked past us 30 minutes ago and we're convinced that they met through their girlfriends and are now secretly in love with each other. Who would've known?

She rested her head onto my shoulder, interlinking our arms and sighed.

"You okay?" I looked down at her.

"I'm perfect. I love this. This and our little people." A smile grew on her face, her head slowly tilting up to make eye contact with me. I placed a gentle kiss on her lips, remaining there for a few seconds before genuinely suddenly contemplating how lucky I've gotten.

"What do you think people would say about us?" She took a bottom lip in between her teeth, blushing.

I paused for a second, trying to conjure up the best way to tell her I'm utterly in love with her without freaking her out.

"I think they would see a beautiful woman, sitting with a man who definitely doesn't deserve her, but is the happiest and luckiest man to ever walk this earth."

She shook her head, smiling like someone seeing the colours of a sunset for the first time before leaning up, hesitating right before our lips joined, and finally making me feel every emotion that I've held in for the last 20 years, right into every kiss.

"What about now?" She murmured against my lips.

"A guy who's extremely flustered every time the love of his life kisses him." I cleared my throat, completely spilling my thoughts. It's like she has some sort of compulsion over me, I can't keep anything to myself around her. It's like she feels like comfort and home just muddled up into one person and I don't have to hide from her. And now she's mine. She knows I've loved her from the moment I laid eyes on her, whether that be the childlike, pre-school love or the love where you can't picture a future without them, I know she knows, but I just can't wait to be the one to finally say it out loud.

"Love of your life, huh, T?" She pulled away, raising her eyebrows, pretending to act shocked.

"Well, there's no one more worthy is there?" I ruffled her

hair, slinking my arm around her neck and pulling her impossibly closer to me.

"You know I wasn't joking about New York. I really want you there, Ellie." I re-introduced the subject.

She sighed, shuffling to sit in front of me, rather than by my side.

"I don't want to say no." She began.

"Then don't." I grabbed her hands, squeezing them.

At the end of the day, if she doesn't want to come, it's not the end of the world. There's just not a soul that I would rather make this step of my life with, a new country, for God knows how long. I missed her so much for the days I was away before, and I've never been involuntarily away from her for more than 2 weeks maybe? It's going to be hell.

"I just, I can't. You're going to be so busy that you won't even realise that I'm not there. I promise. I just don't want to sit alone in a hotel room all day while you're off doing businessy stuff." She shrugged, "We'll facetime all the time. You can give me regular text updates and the time will fly by." She ran her hands up and down my shoulders before pulling me into a hug.

Just as I was about to try and convince her for the last time before giving up, her phone began to buzz in her pocket, removing her warmth from me and adjusting her position to reach for it.

I didn't quite manage to see the caller ID, but Ellie didn't even get a word in after 'Hello' before the voice was frantic. I couldn't make out what it was saying apart from 'I'm sorry'.

"No. No it's okay I promise, I'll come now." She spoke up, shocking me.

She's leaving?

She slung her bag over her shoulder, beginning to stand up, the phone still pressed to her ear as she nodded, giving me a sympathetic 'sorry' look.

I frantically stood up, giving her a confused look, as she, almost reluctantly, hung up the call.

"Who was that? Where are you going?" I followed her quick steps to the park exit.

She paused, without turning to face me, taking a deep breath.

"It was Brady. He needs help with something." She resumed her quick paces.

"Brady?!" My mind went a million different places but he was not one of them. I felt a pang of anger bubble within me, "What happened to 'Brady being a troll as per'," I quoted the last time she mentioned him to me.

"I know, he's just been nice lately, and I owe him a favour or two." She refused to look back at me.

"For what?" I grabbed her arm tightly to completely stop her. She looked stunned between my grip and my undoubtedly angry expression.

"Do you recall that we're currently walking free right now and not rotting in some prison cell, Theo? God. He's just been helpful with everything I'm going through." She gritted her teeth, trying to pull her arm out of my hand.

"Everything you're going through? Since when is that something I can't help you with?" I loosened my grip slightly, allowing her to slip out of it.

"Since you think I'm crazy for it." She muttered, "I have to go. I'll talk to you later." She stormed off without so much of a look back, a wave goodbye or a smile.

It hurt, to see her so defensive over him, to see her jump to his rescue even though we were sitting here together, on a date I would even call it.

She doesn't owe him anything and it's stupid that she thinks that she does.

*I need a drink.*

# Chapter Sixteen

## MILES

I genuinely don't know what I would do without Ellie. I called her out of the blue after being called into a case last minute, completely expecting that she would say she's busy and she turned up anyway. My saviour.

I'm on my way home now after the most tiring shift we've had in a while. I do feel bad for leaving Ellie with Maeve so suddenly for so long too but she was the only available person that I felt okay leaving her with, with no expectation of having to pay her back with something.

It's felt like I've been driving for years, the roads dragging on, prolonging the inevitable facing of her, having to tell her what's happened in this case.

Sitting in the car in the pouring rain, listening to and trying to sift out my own thoughts might seem therapeutic, but that couldn't be further from the truth right now. I can't go into my own home because she is in there, with my daughter, and I cannot bring myself to tell her the truth about tonight. It's 3 in the morning so no doubt they are both asleep but God, what would I do to hear *her* reassure *me* right now. I know that I'm the one who's meant to be reassuring her, telling her that everything will be okay and that she's not absolutely insane, because I know Ellie, and I know that she's not crazy, in fact she's the only reason I stayed sane while she was still on the team. In reality, I don't know how much I'll be able to help her and I'm terrified of that. I made sure she knew that she could come to me if she needed to, but Prescott is breathing down my neck about this and I know the longer I'm aware of this, the worse it's going to be. For the both of us.

The case we got called into tonight? A drowning. A boy was found, drowned, near the sewers. It's been thunder storming all night. Every detail we found, revealed to us, I could hear her entrusting me with her dreams and every one of her thoughts. "*It felt like the air was thick, I couldn't breathe.*" I heard her voice shadow under "Does the air seem a bit thick to you in here?" Prescott said to me in the sewer tunnel. I felt sick with fear, with pain, with confusion. What did she do to deserve this haunting?

Eventually, I got myself out of the car, making a quick jog inside to save myself from getting too wet in the seemingly ever-lasting rain. I crept in my own house, hanging my coat next to hers. That felt...oddly domestic.

I noticed the TV whispering in the background, the subtle sound of small exhales filling the room. There she was, draped over the arm of the sofa, with my little girl curled into the crevice of her waist. With as little as a step, Maeve stirred, glancing up and immediately beaming over to me when she realised who it was, leaving Ellie fast asleep.

"You're home!" She squealed as quietly as she could while containing her excitement.

"Hey, shh, sorry it's so late Mae." I picked her up with my

free hand, her head fitting perfectly in between my neck and shoulder as she got comfortable in her position, "Did you have a nice time with Ellie?" I walked closer to where she resided, watching her chest rise and fall, the soft glow of the moonlight perfectly casted onto her face, almost miraculously.

"Can she come over all the time? We played princesses together, and we also made berry beary cakes!" She pointed over to the kitchen counter where a small rack of cupcakes sat, decorated with frosting, decorated in the shape of a bear with a strawberry hat on. Creative, I'll give her that.

I chuckled under my breath before placing a kiss on Maeve's forehead, "We'll see, okay? Get to bed now, I'll be right there to tuck you in." I placed her down, watching her run off into the hallway. I will never understand how someone can have that much energy at all hours of the day, with or without any specific amount of sleep.

"*Shit, Miles. You're back. I must've fallen asleep, I'm so sorry.*" She gasped, her voice tired and weary.

My heart catapulted at the simplest yet most complicated thing she could've possibly said. My name. She never calls me by my first name apart from the odd occasion where she and Carly are talking about how cold and scary Miles Brady is. The entire office thinks I don't hear anything they talk about but from where my office and desk is I have the perfect view and hearing of everywhere, and I love it. The way my name rolls off of her tongue and echoes into my soul sends chills up my spine. Who would've known her saying something as simple as my name would spiral me into such intense feelings towards her. No matter how hard I trained myself against this, against her, nothing could ever completely erase the connection she would link to in my mind.

"It's okay, Mae was asleep too, she woke up when I got in." I walked over, grabbing and lighting a match to turn on the fireplace and taking a seat next to her as she sat up, rubbing her eyes softly.

"How was work?" She sniffled, still in a sleepy haze.

I paused, knowing that it'll only send her into a spiral if I told her the cold hard truth about the case we worked on. The last thing I want to do is scare her or freak her out even more.

"Tiring. Definitely could've waited until tomorrow." I groaned, flopping my head into my hands.

Lying to Ellie was not something on my recent things to do list. I felt the urge and desire and utter need to protect her, not that she even needs protecting, look at her.

"So...nothing about, you know?" She took a deep breath, making prolonged eye contact with me. Her eyes were wide, staring into mine, expectedly, waiting for the answer that I wasn't going to give her.

"No, nothing. That's good though, right?" I quickly glanced at her, trying to understand how she felt about the situation.

"I don't know... Either it's still to come or that's it, I'm insane. Like, criminally, absolutely, without limit insane. I don't know which would be better, or worse for that fact."

"Easton...Ellie, you're not insane. Far from it. Your mind is a fascinating and unfathomable place, and just because we can't explain it right now, doesn't mean we'll never be able to." I placed my hand over hers, rubbing my thumb over the back of her hand to try and soothe her. I noticed her cheeks flush and she turned to face me with a shocked expression the moment her name slipped out of my mouth. It feels right, right now, it feels personal and true. I no longer have the boundary and the fear of work and our team and I feel like I could... I feel like she could bring me back to the time in my life where I wasn't constantly isolated, or cold, or dismissive. Back to before. Before...everything. I try to be cold and closed and contemptuous because I fear that I'll trap myself into the initial façade of happiness. True happiness. It happened before and that's when I lost... her. And when I lost her, I thought, how could I ever love someone again? How could I ever feel at peace within myself knowing that she loved me and I lost her. Just as I was about to drown under the eternal blanket of guilt, Ellie came wandering into my life, and I saw her. I saw everything that I had lost, reincarnated into this troubled, complicated soul and knew that I couldn't pull her down with me, and so I did the opposite. I pushed her away. Yet here I am, sitting by her side, knowing that no amount of force could've pulled me away from our inevitable connection. The cosmic link to her in my soul, in my mind, within my life was so utterly foreseeable yet so utterly heartbreaking. For months, years on end I felt awful about loving. Loving someone again that death would inescapably brush past. Becoming friends with death forms an unimaginable bond with life, and with life comes love, and God, does she remind me of that feeling all over again.

# Chapter Seventeen

## ELLIE

Hearing my name roll off Brady's tongue so effortlessly felt like the entire world was lit on fire, surrounding, engulfing us with flames yet not allowing either to be singed. Such a small gesture, something so worthless yet uncomplicated, felt like an entire weight lifted from the tension or, maybe awkwardness surrounding us. My heart fluttered at the sound of his voice finally reaching the part of my soul that had failed to be heard from for the last 4 years. I had to refrain myself from sinking into his grasp right then and there. Why does he have to be so goddamn supportive?

I buried my thoughts which were begging me to stay by his side and shuffled away from his grasp, letting the cool air drift between the heat of our hands.

He cleared his throat, shaking his head slightly before sighing and standing up, retreating over to his work bag, "Anyway, I'm sorry again about calling you here so last minute, here." He handed me £200 cash.

"What? No, no, no, I'm not taking your money, Brady." I

pushed it back into his hand and picked up my phone, which was...great, dead, "I really do appreciate it but no." I gave him a weak smile.

"Why not? We can work something out. Of course, if you wouldn't mind babysitting her again, only if you want to, only if you're free I mean, you don't have to." He shoved his hands into his pockets, stumbling over his words before pinching the bridge of his nose and chuckling, shaking his head, "I'm terrible at this."

I smiled at him, feeling like our conversations weren't forced and finally natural. I will never get over this feeling. I could have a million conversations with Miles Brady and I would still feel a new sense of comfort in his presence. Whether that was because of our newfound relationship, this revelation of a bond, or because in my life, I have never felt so unjudged, so at peace in someone's company than his.

"Just...call me, if you need me." I nodded, picking up my still damp jacket, while getting a strong whiff of rain and his cologne from his coat next to mine.

"You too." He ambled over to me, reaching beside me while our faces became all too close to one another as he leant for the door. He paused, mere inches away from me, studying me. His eyes darted from my eyes, to my lips, to my hair, to my cheeks. What is he thinking right now? Does he want to kiss me as much as I want to kiss- hold on. No. I don't want this. I need to leave.

"I should go." I retreated from his grasp and out of the front door just as quickly as my feelings arose in my stomach.

I got into my car, somewhat dry from the rain that was finally easing up, and released a huge built-up sigh. Why does he make me feel this way? I've always been fascinated by him but to the point where it turned into anger, bitterness, not *this*. Not butterflies or blushing when he says my name, or picking up my coat to smell his lingering cologne. *What?* I threw my coat into my backseat in frustration and sped out of his driveway, cranking the volume of the radio to the maximum to drown out thoughts of the wonderfully annoying Miles Brady.

As much as I felt awful for leaving Theo at the park, just as things were taking a step on the right track in terms of... "us", whatever us means. Knowing that Brady is right there, and I'm, unfortunately, at his beck and call, he listens. He cares...? Who knows if he *cares,* he listens. He doesn't make me feel crazy and absolutely nothing, no amount of love and support can match the feeling of being listened to.

F lopping onto my bed and seeing my phone start rapidly buzzing as it sprung back to life sent a surge of panic through me. I've been so on edge ever since, well, ever since everything has started going downhill. I peered at the screen with multiple missed calls and messages from Theo, a message from my therapist and a message from Olivia.

T : *Please answer the phone, I didn't mean to end the night how I did, can I come over?*
*1am*
T: *Els, stop ignoring me, let's talk about this please.*
*2:47am*
T: *For God's sake Ellie where are you? Why aren't you home?*
*3:10am*

. . .

H e came here? Just as I went to type a response, my phone sprung to life with a call, reading Olivia. Why is she calling me at this time?

I reluctantly answered the call, bringing my phone to my ear.

"Hey, Olivia, what's up?" I yawned, trying to make it seem like she just woke me up.

"Hey, Ellie girl! I was just calling to ask you to come and pick up Theo, he came over and he's pretty drunk." She giggled at something his voice muffled from the other end of the room.

My heart sank with so many different concerns and questions arising from the situation. Theo doesn't drink. He *never* drinks. Maybe the occasional champagne for a celebration at dinner and then I have no choice but to drive, but other than that, never. Ever since we got in an accident, while he insisted that he was completely sober I haven't seen him even smell a glass of wine. Long story short, we went to university together, and what kind of experience would it be if we didn't go a week straight partying and drinking. Someone ended up running us off the road, he swerved, crashing us into a tree and giving me a concussion. I was *obviously* fine but he never really trusted himself with the combination of me, alcohol and driving ever again.

I sighed, "Okay. Okay, I'm on my way, send me your address." I scampered out of bed, pulling on a jacket, still with the phone pressed to my ear.

"Els? Ellie, baby. Why didn't you answer me? I miss you." I heard a drunken voice slur through the phone.

"I'm coming, Theo, I'll be there soon." I felt a pang of guilt in my chest echoing the thoughts that it was my fault he was drunk; I wonder what was going through his mind the entire time I was at Brady's house. Of course, I had to be *there with him.* If I didn't jump to his rescue, I would've been there to comfort my boyfriend. Or whatever we are. We act like a couple, we basically are a couple, he's just never officially asked me.

"I'm sorry Ellie, I'm sorry. I thought you him, you with me, no, him and I don't want to lose you and I did something, but I love you and." He sniffled through the line before Olivia took the phone back, without allowing me to say another word.

He was drunk because of me. It was all my fault. I left him alone with his thoughts while I was having the time of my life with my old boss' kid rather than simply just saying I'm busy and spending time with Theo. I'm simply going to brush past the 3 words that he's finally said to me which would be completely normal if we were best friends forever, with no strings attached, but we've not gone down that road simply because of how our fate and destiny has twisted itself. I felt myself sink into sympathy, pity rather than happiness towards his words, knowing that not only am I nowhere near close to feeling the same way for him, but in way too deep to break his heart. Breaking his heart would shatter my own, and as selfish as that sounds, I'm willing to force myself to love him. And as horrible as *that* sounds, I can't be without him. How can someone make me so happy yet so conflicted and guilty at the same time? The worst thing I could ever do, for the both of us, is walk away. I refuse to walk away.

After a 30-minute drive, I walked up to the front door of the address that Olivia sent me, pausing, unable to immediately face the reality of what's going to be behind the door. Without an ounce of hesitation after I knocked the door flung open, like they were right there waiting for me.

A smug smile greeted me, with her hand resting on her hip, looking perfect as ever. Come on, who needs to look that beautiful at 5 in the morning?

"Come in." She gestured me inside, welcoming me into her house. Everything was pristine, whites and beiges and pristine. Nothing out of place, not one speck of dust or a discarded item of clothing, or leftover food on the side. The only thing out of place was the half-asleep man spread over her white sofa and the bottle of Hennessy half spilt over her table and marble floor.

"Oh, Theo," I quickly marched over to him, cupping his face in my hands, rubbing my thumbs over his cheeks causing his eyes to flutter awake.

He glanced around the room, tiredly, then between me and Olivia a couple times and the almost empty bottle on the floor, "*Shit.*" He groaned, "I'm sorry, Els."

He shook his head, leaning straight up and into my arms. I felt Olivia's patronising gaze focus on us but refused to look in her direction.

"You're okay, let's go home." I split myself from our embrace, nodding in his direction, holding his hand and standing up.

"I'll meet you in the car." He still had a slight slur in his voice but was more understandable and stable. I noticed his hazy gaze was now fixated on Olivia.

I nodded, ignoring the obvious elephant in the room, allowing him time to probably just apologise to her.

"Why were you drinking Theo?" I put the car in park after a long drive of nothing but silence as we pulled into his driveway.

He sighed, rubbing his eyes and biting the inside of his

lip, "I'm going to be honest with you, El, the night that you got fired, I lied to you. You came home and I told you that I picked you up but Brady... he actually dropped you home. I was still there from the night before and he walked in with you in his arms all hero-like and it made me feel horrible for not being there for you. I saw the way he was looking at you like he cared so much that you were okay and-"

My eyebrows shot up in surprise, my mouth immediately resulting in dropping open. "You're telling me...Brady. Brady drove and carried me home? The same Brady who was being an arsehole about my job and my badge?" I mustered up the previous anger that I held in my heart for him, as if I wasn't just fawning over his scent which is probably still lingering in the backseat of my car.

"Yes, and ever since then I've been terrified of having a competition with someone for you. Not that you're some prize to be won, but it's just... it's always been just us two and to be honest with you, Els, I'm so lost without you. My life without you is empty and no matter what or who I try to fill it with, nothing... no one compares to you. I can't picture a life without you and it kills me when I'm not surrounded by you. *Fuck,* I'm so lost without you." He still had a mist of alcohol around him, but tears slowly pooling in his eyes. He talked as if he were thinking out loud, holding his head in his hands and muttering under his breath.

He paused, glancing over to me with glassy eyes, making pure, fragile, untouched eye contact with me. My heart plunged to the boy sitting right in front of me, and he felt right. He felt like exactly what I'd been looking for in this exact moment, and rather than me trying to convince myself that he is what I actually wanted, I know that he is. Whether in an hour, or in a day or in a week I feel differently, but his raw emotion pouring out to me really touched a part of my soul which had gone ignored my entire life. I really see him now. Not my best friend, or someone I need to force myself to be in love with if I know what's right for me, but rather someone who's been standing, waiting for me to notice him for our entire lives, the only person who I can strongly say has stayed through thick and thin. He's loved me and cherished and blessed me for so long I can't help but wonder why. He's lost without me, and as much as I hate to admit it, I feel the same way. Without him, I feel aimless, like my home has been struck away from me. That's exactly what he felt like. Home.

Silence filled the thick air around us, suddenly feeling more golden than dull. Nothing but his shaky, scattered breaths and what might as well be the drumbeat of both of our hearts beating in sync.

"T, you have a place in my heart that no matter what happens, no one else would be able to replace. I wouldn't choose anyone else to spend the last 20 years with. And the next however long you can tolerate me for." I chuckled, taking his cheek into the palm of my hand.

A very brief silence echoed between us before his dimples pierced his cheeks, "Do you remember when we were little, and we used to sit in my parents garden, on the swing set, making up our own stories about how each star was put into the sky, and how the moon was definitely made of cheese?" He laughed throatily before returning to a serious expression, "You know, on every star in that sky, I wished for you. Every time."

In that very moment my smile collapsed, not out of disappointment or being upset, but because hearing those words made my entire body *shut down.* He wished on every star in the sky for *me?* I couldn't concentrate on anything but him at this given moment and the heat escalated between us. I noticed his eyes flick between mine and my lips, leaning slightly further in.

I sprung forward into his slow paced lean, unable to wait a

second longer for him to hesitate and regret his decision, or maybe me with mine, pressing our lips together, kissing him. I paused slightly before feeling him melt into my touch, pulling me closer, desperate for a closer connection. He tugged at my clothes, gravitating my body closer to his before sliding his chair back and slinging me onto his lap in one swift movement. Our lips parted for a second, both left swollen and leaving us gasping for air. All we could look at was one another, frantically, desperately looking into each other's eyes, yearning for some kind of clarity to the speed in which this happened.

He grazed my cheek with his hand before sliding down the side of my neck, gripping my chest and then landing and stopping on my waist.

"You're so beautiful." He kissed me slowly.

I pulled back slightly finally able to breathe without using him as a second source of air, taking a deep breath.

I felt like I had to look at him in an entirely new light. Like I couldn't say his name the same way that I used to, it wouldn't roll off my tongue the same way. We jumped a certain boundary and there was no going back. Part of me is screaming at me to run, trying my best to go back to how we were before the most passionate kiss I've ever experienced in my life, but the way I feel and the way it made me feel says enough. No going back, only diving head first into this new era of us.

## Chapter Eighteen

### ELLIE

"It's lovely to see you again, Ellie. How are things?" She spoke out, her voice her usual calm tone.

"Things are good...things are amazing actually." I blushed to myself.

Theo finally actually made us official last night after the whole car shenanigan. The moment the tables completely flipped and knocked me round the face. Consider the attachment I already had and magnify it by 10 because now that the switch has actually flipped in my brain that Theo loves me, in that way, and he's my boyfriend? It's like we're even more inseparable than we were.

"So, since our last session, how have you been? In terms of everything." She turned to a clean page in her notebook and got her pen ready to write.

I sighed, taking a deep breath, "It's actually been pretty good, I've only had one vision since our last session, and hopefully it stays that way. I actually am in a relationship now." I smiled to myself, "With Theo. I started babysitting...for Brady. Things are going quite well."

She nodded silently and took a minute to jot down some notes. *I think I would genuinely kill* to know what she's writing in there.

"That's great. I'm very happy for you, Ellie," She smiled, "If we could stray away from this and back onto your visions, tell me more about them, how you feel, how you subconsciously react..." She resumed her serious expression.

If I could get through this without starting to panic that would be amazing. I've been thinking about them quite a lot recently, considering the last vision I had, didn't actually come true. I made Brady swear to tell me if it did come true, and he hasn't, so I'm giving myself and my brain the all clear, "Well, they were all about different things, but I always woke up in a cold sweat, breathless, a bit disorientated, maybe a little dizzy, I don't know. It's hazy." I tried recalling the emotions I felt in my most vulnerable moments, only to feel myself start going back to that place. As much as I can think about it over and over again, the second it comes out of my mouth it's as if it becomes real again, it forms a presence.

"You mentioned in your forms that you were a detective, correct?" I nodded in response, "Have you considered this as an internal case of PTSD? A lot of the time, you might think everything is okay, but your brain has a funny, different way of telling you that it isn't."

"Aren't you meant to be the one to be able to tell me that?" my face scrunched in confusion, not meaning to sound rude or backhanded but slightly coming off that way, "I mean, like, you're a therapist."

"Of course, but I can only help you with what you tell me, and you're not telling me much." She said blankly, calling me out.

"Right, right, sorry." I pinched my eyes together. Therapy was always such a taboo thing in my family. But I guess the fact that the people who I considered family were absolutely deranged didn't help.

"Why don't we go back in time a little bit, tell me about your childhood, your family, if that's okay with you of course." She suggested just as the thought popped into my head. Great. I will go years and years trying to avoid talking about my family to anyone. I don't think Theo even knows every gruesome detail about them. I would rather get run over a million times over than talk about them, but, as reluctant I am, she's right. She can only help me if I tell her everything, and as much as I try to recall everything, there always feels like there's something missing.

"I guess it all went downhill when my mum, Lizzie, started doing drugs. I was only 8 and it was rough, I mean, it was more than rough but it was just... eye opening, I guess. She used to take me to her meetings with her so I could collect all her sober stickers, 'I'm getting sober for my baby' she used to say, and we'd go home and she'd tell me she was proud of me, then she'd open a bottle of wine and a bottle of pills and conk out on the sofa until 5pm the next day." I took a deep breath, before continuing, realising the tears brewing in my eyes but refusing to let them overflow, "My dad, Freddy, he was in the marines, so he wasn't around a lot anyway and when he came home one day and found myself trying to make us both a grilled cheese toastie for dinner while she was unconscious on the sofa, he wasn't very happy. Their marriage was struggling as it was and after he found out she was taking me to meetings with her and she wasn't sober it just completely fell apart and it stayed like this for...maybe 4 years? I don't really remember the time frames. Next thing I know, my dad took me to my Aunt Willow's house indefinitely until my mum was sober again. Of course, she claimed she was and regained custody of me when I was 14, until...well, she- she overdosed. She-she died." I felt myself choke on the word and a knot formed into my throat, the tears no longer threatening, but instead pouring out of my eyes without consent.

This entire time my therapist was looking at me with this pitiful, sympathetic look. I hate it. The few people who have heard this story in one sitting from start to finish have always given me the 'I'm so sorry' look as if that will do anything about it, or to help me in any way.

"Sorry." I cleared my throat, excusing the tears which were streaming down my cheeks, flushing them a hot red.

"Take your time, Ellie. I can appreciate that this is difficult to talk about." She smiled pitifully.

I nodded, already wanting to get up and leave this godforsaken room, "After a year with my dad, he couldn't take any more time off and so he went back to the marines, sold the house, and I went to live with my aunt permanently this time. A week after I turned 16, my auntie got into a car accident and had to stay in hospital for a while so I stayed with Theo and his family. At this point, they were quite aware of everything that happened in my house and so they welcomed me with open arms. It was like living in a dream while I was there. You could really feel the love as soon as you walked into a room and it was envious, I was... jealous, to say the least. Anyway, my auntie ended up passing away when I was 18 and my dad eventually came back, and because he was in the marines, I somehow got this scholarship for university to do law and criminology and... well the rest is present day history."

Part of me is completely desensitised to some of the most traumatic events that have ever happened in my life, and the other part of me is begging me to let the rest of the dam crack open and let the floodgates of emotion pour through. I don't think I'd be able to listen to the second part of my brain, because that means coming to terms with it, and coming to terms with it means feeling, and going through the grief process all over again, and I just don't think I can do that right now. I don't think I would be able to remember everything and survive it.

"Thank you for telling me everything, and I'm sorry that you had to go through all of that at such a young age." She handed me a box of tissues which were ready and prepared on the table in the corner of the room.

I took a few, dabbing my eyes and my cheeks dry before taking a deep breath. Feeling just slightly embarrassed about my physical reaction to all this, as if this isn't my life and I shouldn't be accustomed to it.

"Are you still in contact with your father now?" She questioned, making me realise I know absolutely nothing about where he is today.

"No, I-uh haven't spoken to him since I graduated." I shrugged.

"What about your family history? For example, having premonitions or predictions about the near future might be hereditary."

"Also, a no." I admitted, suddenly growing curious to what she was talking about, "You really think my family could be the reason why I'm having visions?" I leant forward, intrigued.

"Perhaps, a lot of fortune tellers or psychics come from a long line of people like themselves. Maybe you should look into that, it may help with elements of your life such as closure or resolution. All of your visions may stem from your lack of understanding of your family and why you were treated the way that you were as a child. Feelings which surface in the form of something more dangerous." She explained.

I link certain feelings with my visions, drowning and suffocation, disgust, sickness, not being able to see what was right in front of me, she could be right.

I took in what she said, slightly surprised that I never put two and two together myself. She's right, and a new burst of curiosity suddenly sprung through me.

"You think I should get into contact with my Dad?" Not really asking, but rather pondering to myself, not knowing whether or not that would be the right decision.

"If you think that is the right decision, then yes."

I groaned as I walked in the front door, alerting Theo of my presence, and immediately was hit with the most beautiful smell in the entire world. Food. I slung my bag off of my shoulder and took my shoes off leaving them messily scattered about the hallway and followed the smell almost into the kitchen before Theo came running out to greet me.

"You're back!" He panted, looking over his shoulder and back at me, sweating.

"Yeah, I am." I chuckled, placing a kiss on his cheek, "You miss me?" I tried to walk past him but he blocked me, smiling nervously.

"Always. I just- let me cover your eyes, okay?" He took the tea towel that was slung over his shoulder and quickly wrapped it around my eyes, taking me off guard and leading me into our dining room.

He pulled out a chair, guiding me into my seat and tucking me in.

"Okay, ready?" He sighed, with a slight tremble in his tone.

"Mhm." I felt myself blushing already, scared at what surprise was on the other side of my vision.

He slowly untied the towel, revealing our usually wooden dining table covered with a white and red table cloth, a bouquet of red roses placed in a vase in the centre with a small rectangular box as he placed down a tray of lasagne as my eyes readjusted to the light.

My jaw dropped open in shock as I looked between his proud grin and the table over and over again.

"Theo, what- what is this?" A smile uncontrollably spread across my face making my cheeks glow even more than they were already.

"Ta-da! Lunch for two." He sat down opposite me, dishing us both out a portion, still having that cheesy, adorable grin planted on his face.

"You really didn't have to." I dug in almost immediately, it tasting just as delicious as every other meal he's made for me.

"You're right. But you're my girlfriend and I wanted to do something sweet for you." He tugged off his apron, laying it over the back of his chair, "Open your present." He slid the black box on the table towards me.

"Is this what was for 'future us'?" I bounced in my seat, excitedly, remembering the gift he put aside on my birthday.

"No, this is something else."

I shuffled open the lid, revealing the most beautiful, dainty, Swarovski crystal bracelet I've ever seen in my life. I immediately dropped the box on the table to bring my hands up to cover my mouth in shock, my eyes instinctively brimming with tears.

"My God, this is beautiful, how did you- why did you- thank you." I glanced back up at him with glassy eyes.

"Here, let me put it on you." He came round to my side and took my wrist into his hand, carefully clipping and then admiring the crystal on my hand, before reaching up to me and placing a prolonged kiss on my temple.

After a brief, comfortable silence, the smell of burning filled the air quite quickly, causing us to both spin around to the direction of the kitchen.

"Shit. Shit, shit, shit." Theo ran towards the oven, opening the door and taking a tray of... black circles...? out, "I burnt them." He sighed defeatedly.

"Forgive me, but what are they meant to be?" I tried to hide my chuckle to stop him from feeling bad.

"I tried to make macarons, your favourite, but clearly I need to stick to cooking and not baking." He scraped the macarons off and placed the smoking tray in the sink and ran cold water over the top.

"I'm sure they aren't that bad... just burnt." I smelt one, instantly being greeted by a foul stench and dropping it instantly.

He pressed his lips together to suppress his laugh, "I must've forgotten something." He let out a laugh.

"You're such a Dory." I quickly came around to the other side of the counter, tipping the 'macarons' into the bin, and that's when it hit me, "Oh my God." I spun round to face him, laughing already at my mind's connections.

"What? Why're you laughing?" He smiled confusedly.

Trying to console myself but not being able to subdue my laugh, "You're a Dory? Theo-Dory? My God, that's genius." I cackled, slapping him on the arm.

"Please, I beg you not to make that a thing." He slapped his hands over his eyes, shaking his head, still laughing.

It's moments like these where I think I could stay here forever. Laughing in the kitchen with my best friend- my boyfriend, about stupid little nicknames and absolute nothing-ness, but radiating just pure joy and belly aching laughs.

"Whatever you say, Dory," I said, still through fits of giggles, slinking my arms around his shoulders and peppering kisses on either of his cheeks, "Next time leave the baking to me, okay?"

He effortlessly picked me up, placing me on the kitchen counter and beaming up to me, like a little kid in a candy store,

"Perfect, I cook, you bake. We're a match made in heaven." He bit his bottom lip scanning my features, propping himself slightly up and placing a tender kiss onto my lips, hovering less than an inch away from me and pecking my lips again.

"We should finish dinner." I hopped off the counter, skipping back to the dining table and retaking my seat.

"You realise that we didn't finish talking about New York the other day." He cleared his throat, joining me back at the dinner table.

Just as I was about to speak my phone started pinging rapidly in an explosion of texts. It's like fate didn't want us to talk about New York, ever. I quickly peered to the side and saw already 10 messages from Carly.

"I should get that." I grabbed my phone reading through the frantic texts.

"Wait, before you run off. I have an event at my restaurant and I get a plus one... I would rather not go at all than go without you. Come with me?" He grabbed my free hand.

"Yeah. Yeah, that'd be lovely." I smiled slightly.

"Are we ever going to talk about New York?" He asked pleadingly.

"Maybe someday." I shrugged, trying to brush it off and texting back Carly, "It's a frie-mergency. I have to go."

"You always do." He sighed.

"I know. I'm sorry, I'll make it up to you I promise." I placed a gentle kiss on his cheek, grabbing my bag again and heading out the front door.

" I just... haven't seen you in a while, that's all." She buried her face into her hot chocolate.

I looked at her suspiciously, not understanding why the texts were so frantic if she just wanted to see me again.

"Are you sure? It sounded like you had something urgent to say." I took a sip of mine, eyeing her over the top of my mug.

"Mhm! You know, quick catch up, we can talk about my birthday party, etcetera. Now update me on everything." She smiled, extremely forcibly, whilst also reminding me it's her birthday soon, making a mental note to properly talk to her about that when she wasn't acting so weird.

"Okay. Well, I'm a taken girl. Theo finally asked me out." I blushed, now me being the one hiding my face.

Carly's jaw dropped open, spilling her drink slightly. She patted her chin dry, clearing her throat, "Theo?"

"Yes, why is that a surprise, I-"

"No, it's not! I just-" She shrugged, avoiding eye contact.

Everything about her was off today, either she was hiding something or she knew something.

"Carly..." I said in a warning tone.

"*Querida*," She warned.

"You forget that I know you-"

"I think I have feelings for Lucas." She spat out, holding her head in her hands.

"Parker?!" I choked on a marshmallow. Considering the last time that we spoke she said 'Puh-lease' to the thought of *him* having feelings for *her* is absolutely crazy, "You're joking, right?"

"I know you two have a weird thing going on and you can slap me if I'm being an absolute *pendeja,* but I haven't acted on it and he's just been so romantic and cute recently and I just..." She finally took a breath.

"Carly." I took a deep breath, purposefully prolonging the

silence so that I scared her a little, "I can't believe... you haven't told me this! Spill everything, I swear, this is so exciting." I clapped my hands, grabbing hers across the table.

She exhaled, clearly relieved at my reaction, "He brings me flowers every day, even on my days off, he leaves them on my desk with a little handwritten note. We went out to a bar with a couple of others and it just felt like there was absolutely nobody else there. He picks me up, drops me home. He's such a gentleman, he's started to keep a spare hair tie on his wrist because I'm always complaining that I don't have one...he's just a little sweetheart." She brought her hands to her cheeks, trying to hide her enormous smile.

I felt my eyes tearing up, in just complete happiness that my best friend has found someone who will treat her the way that she deserves to be treated. If you would've told me that was Lucas Parker, maybe I wouldn't have slept with him, *but,* nevertheless, I'm happy for her. She deserves someone like him in her life.

"Enough about me." She cleared her throat, still visibly giggly, "Care to tell me why Mr. Brady has been awfully cheerful recently?" She tilted her head to the side like an excited puppy.

"What? No...that's not because of me." I bit my lip, my leg subconsciously bouncing under the table. Carly returned to me with a look that pretty much said 'I don't believe in your bullshit'.

"Fine, but you can't tell *anyone.* Okay?"

"I will definitely be telling Lucas. But I'll make sure he keeps his lips *shut.*" She bounced in her chair.

"Okay. He's been helping me out. A lot. With-" The realisation suddenly sprung on me that Carly doesn't know about my visions. Maybe only the first one and I'd like to leave that in the 'workplace gossip' sector of my life, "With some work stuff.

And- Okay this is the bit that needs to be kept hush. I've been *babysitting* for him. He has a daughter, Carly."

"*No me diga.* You're kidding." Her jaw hung wide enough to almost hit the floor.

"Dead serious. Her name's Maeve and she's just the most adorable soul on this earth." I smiled over Brady's little girl.

"Not the update I was expecting, but you never disappoint, do you?" She grinned excitedly; jaw still open slightly.

"Never." I smiled proudly, laughing and shaking my head at her excitement, "Okay. Your birthday. What do you want?"

"Your presence. I'm having a little party, and of course, you're coming. I won't be taking no for an answer." She clapped enthusiastically.

# Chapter Nineteen

## ELLIE

From where I stood, the world was indistinguishable. A hazy blur of a dull grey sky merging in with the dull grey earth. Maybe I was getting my colours mixed up, I couldn't focus on anything. It's as if the entire world was spinning, but the entire world was the same colour, the same 4 walls, the same dusty, speckly dirt, sprinkling over the bridge of my nose. It left a slight tingle where it laid, slowly progressing, spreading the feeling across my face, the weight of it dropping more and more.

And that's when the last bit of light vanished from my vision, forcing my other senses to take control.

My fingertips came to life, reaching out to my sides and suddenly realising how enclosed the space I was in was. The walls barely stretched an inch of either side of my body, the roof barely an inch above my nose. The second I opened my mouth I felt an endless stream of dirt flow in, choking me, completely drying my mouth out. I tried to scream but the noise ricocheted back into my own ears, vibrating against the box that I was trapped inside.

I used the last ounces of the strength in my arms to pound against the roof, begging, wishing for some kind of movement to break me free from the darkness, but only for it to fall in on me, turning everything dark. Unmistakably, God knows how, but darker than it was before. Nothing would move. No strength remained in my arms for a push, I had no voice remaining for a final scream, a final push, a final help. Silence surrounded me, consumed me, controlled me. Darkness, and silences.

I gasped for air, my entire body immediately jolting upright, my hand instinctively clawing at my chest in order to get some sort of hold on the fact that I was alive, physically here. I wasn't in a box, surrounded by dirt... I wasn't buried alive. My throat was dry, desperate for something to prove to my brain that I hadn't just swallowed a mouthful of dirt.

Grabbing the glass of water from my bedside, I quickly noticed a note balanced against my lamp, written '*Call me when you're up – T*'.

I quickly picked up my phone, desperate to distract myself from yet another disturbing vision that my brain had morphed into consciousness and clicked his number, him answering within less than 3 rings.

"Morning, Baby, how'd you sleep?" Theo's voice burst through the phone.

"Mhm, okay." Was all I was able to make out through my grogginess, sipping my water.

"I didn't want to wake you before I left, thought I'd let you get some rest." He cleared his throat, obviously wanting to talk about something.

Normally, here is where I would be appreciative of him

letting me sleep, but that darkness and silence is the last thing on earth that I ever want to do again right now.

"Why'd you want me to call you?" I croaked.

"Okay, well I was thinking about solutions for New York." He started, I immediately flopped back into bed, not wanting to focus on something like this right now.

"T, can we talk about this later?" I groaned.

"No, because later will never happen and you know it." He firmly stated, continuing without letting me say another word, "I know you don't have a job, and if you're worried about spending money that you don't have or anything like that, you don't have to be! After New York, there'll be enough money coming in and neither of us will have to work full-time. It'll be great for us!" I could practically envision the dimples popping out of his cheeks and could hear the grin on his face.

"So, you want me to be completely financially dependent on you?" I stated in the dullest voice possible to let him know this is the worst idea he could possibly ever have.

"Well, I'm just saying, there's no reason for you to say no anymore."

"But I already told you, I'm not going because you're going to be busy anyway, and I do have a job now, so I'll talk to you later." I hung up the phone out of pure anger.

I appreciate that he's desperate for me to come with him but who knows why? He's never going to see me anyway and he'll be back before we both know it, so it doesn't even matter. The only issue is, now I have to find a job, or get my job back because I just couldn't keep my big mouth shut from a little white lie, could I?

I sighed, smashing my pillow against my face and groaned into it, before flinging myself out of bed and getting ready. I need to go and talk to Brady about my messed-up brain and everything that it creates, and if I'm lucky do some severe convincing.

"He's off, at a funeral of a victim." Prescott coldly brushed past me asking where Brady was.

My heart sank at his words, crushing my every organ on the way down.

"What?" I managed to stutter out, following his quick paces down the hall, "He can't be, no this isn't happening." My mind flashed between the scenes of my vision and the thought of Brady possibly burying someone alive.

I span on my heel, ready to make a bee line for the exit to try and find Brady, and lo and behold him already towering over me.

"Brady." I gasped, trying to catch my breath, looking up at his deadpan expression.

"Easton." He nodded, staring down at me, hesitating to break eye contact before glancing up at Prescott.

"I had another vision." I whispered breathlessly, grabbing his forearm in a panic, "I think someone's going to get buried alive and I-"

"Buried alive?" Prescott's voice boomed from behind me, startling me. A boisterous chuckle echoing down the hall, "You truly are crazy Miss Ellie." He shook his head.

"She's not crazy." Brady spoke back.

I gave him a tight-lipped smile before turning back to Prescott, "If you just hear me out, if weird murders keep happening while I'm on the team, we'll have a head start. You'll see it when I see it and you'll be able to solve it before it even happens!" I begged him. I needed this job back, maybe, it would give me some of my sanity back too.

"I don't care who I have to tell, or what I have to do to get this into your clearly insane brain, you are not, getting your job back in this team." He enunciated every other word.

"Don't talk to her like that." Brady stepped past me, squaring up to Prescott.

"Be careful where you step, Miles." He taunted.

"Remember *Prescott,* you need me more than I need this place. Trust me." He prodded his shoulder, turning around, grabbing my shoulder and pushing me to walk in front of him towards his office.

"I'm sorry about him." He sat down behind his desk and sighed, "Why're you here? I told you to call-"

"I know. I know, I just panicked and I thought this would be quicker than just waiting on you to answer the phone." I shook my head, "I'm sorry."

"Don't be." He leant forward on his desk, holding eye contact with me, "I have a question." He cleared his throat, opening the draw next to him and bringing out a notebook, sliding it towards me on the table, all while his eyes pierced into my soul.

I nodded, albeit a bit too enthusiastically.

"I shouldn't be doing this." He shook his head, sighing, "I was briefed about specifically not doing this." He knocked his fist against the table.

"You were briefed about me? I'm flattered." I tried to hide the smile growing on my face.

He shook his head again, laughing slightly.

"Work with me. For me." He swallowed visibly, "What I mean, is... you can write down all your visions, in as much detail as possible and you can help me out with researching anything to do with the crimes. Prescott can't know about this.

But I am fully aware of how stupid it would be not to include you in these."

I paused, just purely stunned at his offer. I immediately knew that I wanted to take it without hesitation, my nodding showed him that.

"Yes." I took a deep breath, with a mix of nodding, shaking my head, laughing, taking breaths, "Yes, thank you, I don't know what else to say." I smiled at him.

"It's the least I can do. Maeve keeps asking when she's next going to see you." He broke into a real smile, chuckling, "She's obsessed with you."

My cheeks went hot at his comment, my gaze averting into my lap.

"You haven't told anyone about her... have you?" He questioned.

Just as I was about to speak up and tell him I hadn't, the main culprit herself burst into his office, just as surprised to see me as I was at her outburst.

"Oh, hey babe! Fancy seeing you here!" Her worried look immediately dropped as she skipped over to hug me, then realising why she came in, "Sorry Sir, I didn't mean to just barge in but-"

"What is it, Miss Montana?" He looked up at her expectantly.

"Agent Prescott's requested you in the meeting room, I think Michigan State's team is in there too."

He nodded, heading for the door immediately, "I'll be in contact, Easton." He spoke before leaving Carly and I in his office.

"What on earth are you doing in Miles Brady's office, you cheeky thing?" She nudged me on the shoulder.

"I was just talking to him about getting a job back, he said that there's nothing he can do for me though." I shrugged, standing up and heading for the door.

"You forget that I know you, but I'll get it out of you eventually!" She called after me, walking out of his office and making my way back to my car.

# Chapter Twenty

## ELLIE

It's quite embarrassing how excited I am that I have a job again. Like, disgustingly excited. It definitely doesn't have *anything* to do with the fact that Brady was so willing to give me a job and it's like he had it ready for me! I'll get to babysit Maeve, busy myself with work, inside and outside of the visions, and Theo leaves soon so all my focus will be on work again. It'll be nice to get back into the flow of things, regain some structure in my life. I dropped my bag onto the floor by the front door, skipping into the front room to see Theo's clothes neatly laid out in piles on the sofa, and him retreating out of the bathroom with a bag of toiletries.

"Is that everything you have here?" I picked up a pile, moving it to the side, making room for me to sit down on the sofa.

"Yeah, I've pretty much packed everything that I need at home, surprisingly I have more here." He chuckled, leaning over to me and placing a kiss on my cheek, "Where have you been?"

"Just running some errands, just things I needed to get

done." Which is half true. They were errands, I had to get them done eventually, just not necessarily for me. I know that Theo's just going to overthink me working with *him*, but it would be even worse to not tell him at all. Today was the huge event at Theo's restaurant and God forbid if I brought anything up to him to ruin tonight for us so I might as well just wait until later. Out of pure convenience.

"You pick your dress up from the shop?" He asked, slightly distracted at his packing.

"Mhm, I actually decided on the red one that you wanted rather than the purple one." I gave him a nudge on his shoulder, retreating back out towards my car to get the dress.

"How much luckier could I get?" He threw me a smile, laughing.

"Just... hold on! I'm almost...done!" I struggled at pulling on my zipper without getting my hair caught in it.

"Just let me help you." Theo called from outside the bathroom, knocking repeatedly on the door.

"You're not meant to see your date before the date! It's bad luck." I groaned.

"That's marriage! Not a date. Just open up." He laughed, rattling the doorknob.

"Fine." I rolled my eyes, giving up and unlocking the door.

His smile instantly disappeared when I emerged from the door, showing off what I was wearing.

"I knew I liked the dress but holy-" His gaze snaked down my body, taking in every curve, every tiny detail of the dress.

It had a corset fitted bodice which stopped at my hips, flowing out and draping against the floor.

"Is it nice enough?" I did a small twirl, trying to not trip or come out of the dress.

"You look- wow, there's no words to describe it. You're perfect."

I blushed, turning my back to face him and flinching slightly as his hands came into contact with my lower back.

"Sorry, my hands are cold." He chuckled nervously; I could feel his breath on the back of my neck.

He pushed my hair to one side, running his fingers along my spine as he dragged my zip up.

I inhaled sharply, trying to stop the chills from rising up from his touch.

As he finished zipping me up, he paused with his hands now resting on my shoulders and turned us to face the mirror.

"Look at us. We match perfectly." A smile twisted onto his lips as he adjusted the red handkerchief tucked into his suit pocket.

"Don't we just." I smiled, a blush rising onto my cheeks.

"One last thing before we go." He disappeared out of the bathroom quickly.

I peered out of the bathroom door, watching him rummage through his bag and turn to face me suddenly, hiding something behind his back.

"Come here then." He cocked his head to the side, gesturing me over to him.

I picked up the bottom of my dress, shuffling over to him trying not to trip over my undone heels.

I took a breath, closing my eyes and holding out the palms of my hands and smiling expectantly.

"This one's for future us." He stuttered, I could hear him audibly swallow, flipping over my hand and sliding something onto my finger.

My eyes flicked open, diverting my gaze from him to the ring which glimmered on my right hand. A silver band dotted with diamonds and an T engrained on the back side of the ring.

"I didn't know whether to put a T...or, or an E, because I don't want you to think I put a T because like...I own you or something, it's not like that."

"It's beautiful." I interrupted him, slinging my arms around his neck and pulling him into a hug.

I pulled away from him, admiring the ring on my finger, trying to hide my smile to myself.

"We should go, we're going to be late." He knelt down in front of me, "Here." Looking up at me expectantly.

I looked at him, confused for a second, before he pulled my foot up to balance on his knee, almost making me lose my balance slightly. He adjusted my heel on my foot and started tightening the strap on my ankle, brushing his hand further up my leg and doing the next shoe.

"Thank you." I reached down, helping him up as he brushed himself off, "Let's go."

"Oh, it's so lovely to see you again, honey." Theo's mum came up, hugging me tightly.

"It's nice to see you too, Marnie." I squeezed her back.

"How's work going?" She kept her hand on my shoulder, giving me a sweet smile.

Theo jumped in, saving the conversation and slinging an arm around me, "Hi, Ma." He smiled, keeping an arm around me whilst placing a kiss on her cheek.

Marnie looked between him and I, her eyebrows raising slightly and a smile creeping onto her lips before Stephen came creeping up behind her.

"I just helped myself to those little canapes over there, how wonderful! Very proud of you, son." He spat out with a mouthful of finger food, "Ellie, darling, it's lovely seeing you here."

I nodded through a smile, glancing up at Theo whose eyes were already on me with a smirk pressed onto his lips, "Wanna get some air?" He gestured to the back door near the kitchen.

T took a deep breath, allowing the cold air to invade me and cool me down.

"You okay?" He placed his hand in mine, rubbing his thumb on the back of my palm.

I nodded, looking at him with tears brimming my eyes.

Of course, I'm so overwhelmingly happy for him, seeing his success in person, standing next to him whilst everyone congratulated him was so fulfilling, even on my behalf, knowing he's this amazing successful person and that he's chosen me. But, part of me, the selfish part, is self-conscious. Upset. Putting myself down because of the success of others around me. I know that's not the best thing to do but I just can't help it. All the love and support and endless congratulations that he gets for just being him, I can't help but feel...isolated. Different. I don't belong in this world, and I don't think I ever will.

At this point, the thought of my new job resurfaced in my head, knowing I should tell him, knowing that this whole event was just a convenient opportunity to put off the inevitable bad news.

"I got a job," I spat out before convincing myself to change my mind and not tell him at all.

"You already told me on the phone before you hung up on me earlier." Theo cleared his throat, pausing in his tracks, "So, no New York?"

It completely slipped my mind that I had lied to him on the phone earlier, and honestly it was complete and utter luck that

Brady actually did end up giving me the job, otherwise I would be in absolute deep shit right now.

I sighed as heavily as I possibly could, "New York has been a no since you first brought it up." I stood up, now standing above him, looking down at him sitting on the back door step.

"But I've given you solutions! Why don't you want to-"

"Why are you pushing it so much? I just don't want to!" I shook my head at him.

"Ellie. Money isn't an issue for me, I can cover both of us and you know it." He shot me a condescending look, while standing up, meeting my gaze.

My jaw dropped at his sentence. Money isn't an issue for me either. Yes, I was unemployed for a while but does the man think I would really fall into crippling debt if I lost my job? It's almost as if nobody could get as rich and successful as he is, God forbid I could actually take care of myself.

"This is ridiculous and quite frankly something that just doesn't need to happen. I told you; I'm not being financially dependent on you." I scoffed, in shock at his ignorance and persistence.

"And I told you that I don't know how long I will be gone for. Does seeing me mean absolutely nothing to you?" He took my hand, gripping it firmly, using his other hand to gesture how upset he was.

"You know that's not true. I just don't see the point in me being there with you. You'll be busy 24/7 and back before you know it." I tried reassuring him, sensing the heat rising in this conversation.

"You don't see the point of trying to make this work then." He smiled patronisingly,

"That's not what I said, Theo." I spoke through gritted teeth, his tone cutting away at my last nerve.

"Okay. So, tell me, who are you working for?" He crossed his arms, leaning forward slightly.

My heart dropped, a knot forming in my throat, "You can't be mad at me for getting a job with him." I spoke, knowing that he definitely already knew the answer to his own question.

"I *fucking* knew it." He slammed his hand onto the wall, pacing behind me and towering over me, "So he's why you're staying?"

I pause, giving him a deadpan look, "Do you want me to say yes or something? Because you aren't going to take no for an answer, are you?" I crossed my arms, shifting my weight onto one foot.

He took a deep breath, running his hands through his hair and sighing, "You're right, I'm sorry." He shook his head, leaning his back against the wall.

I ran my hands over my head and rested them on my neck, rolling my eyes slightly. When is it acceptable for me to be sick of all these apologies when all he does is lose his temper all over again?

"This isn't working. Clearly." I finally gained the breath to say.

"What? No, no, no, we're fine. We'll be fine." He rushed over to me, grabbing my arms, and running his hands down them.

"No, Theo, we aren't. You're leaving and you aren't happy with me working with Brady, so we should just...go back to how we were. It was perfect then. When you get back, we'll see where things go but for now, it's just bad timing." I held his hands back, actually wanting to attempt to leave this on a good note. Just friends or in a relationship, I need Theo in my life and he's been such a constant that I'm just not ready to completely let that go.

Part of me felt awful for springing him on this suddenly.

Part of me, the jealous, selfish part of me, was happy that he was aware of my imperfection. Him and I and our true incompatibility. I will never fit into his perfect world of big dinner events and fancy dress, and he will never fit into my havoc and disorganised life.

He nodded. We stood in silence for a minute or so, taking in each other's presence for a final time. A mutual understanding that this was it. As much as we can both just smile and wave goodbye, pretending that we didn't try to be anything more than just friends, pretending that we are just as close as when we started, pretending that everything will be okay. *Deep* down we know that's not the case.

I fiddled with the ring on my finger, about to take it off and hand it back to him.

"Keep it. Please." He held the ring on my hand, kissing it, holding my hand against his lips, lingering for a second, and retreating back into the restaurant.

# Chapter Twenty-One

## ELLIE

"Is it too much?" Carly twiddled in her dress; her lip tucked in between her teeth.

"It's your birthday, there's no such thing as too much." I fixed the strap on her shoulder, twisting her to face me, "You look stunning." I squealed in excitement.

"Well, good, everyone's going to be here in 10-" she was interrupted by the doorbell ringing excessively.

We both smiled at each other, running downstairs and swinging open the door.

Lucas went to step in with a beautifully wrapped present and an extravagant bow on top before pausing in his tracks, his eyes settling on Carly.

He stuttered over his words, trying to spit something out, "Happy birthday." He coughed, drool practically trickling out of his mouth.

"Need a tissue?" Carly smirked, bringing him into a tight hug, laughing.

"You look amazing, happy birthday." He handed her the present, blinking in awe.

"You already said that, but thank you." She kissed his cheek, taking the present from his grasp and sauntering off to the other side of the room.

He swayed idly, turning to face me with a shocked look, "I need a drink. Coming?" He hooked my arm, pulling me along towards the kitchen.

"Let's get you that drink." I laughed.


A champagne cork popped, everyone reacting in cheers and claps. Lucas and I were squeezed into a corner, watching at least 10 people pour through every minute, Carly mingling and laughing with every last one.

Lucas leant against me murmuring something inaudible over the loud music before a screeching feedback noise bounced off the walls, attracting all of our attention onto Carly.

"Hello! Hello! Can everyone hear me!" Carly shouted into the microphone, standing on a chair, almost wobbling off.

Scattered 'yeah' and cheers echoed throughout the room, a few claps encouraging her speech.

"Thank you all *so* much for coming, I just wanted to hop on here and say a few words." She encouraged a cheer, the whole room erupting into applause.

Carly's voice muffled as my hearing focused on Lucas' whispers next to me.

"Ellie, can I tell you something?" He slurred; his eyes still focused on Carly's flamboyant movements on her makeshift stage.

"What is it?" I turned to face him, a gleeful look spread across his face, his pupils heavily dilated, whether from the obscene amount of alcohol he's had, or the view he has, who knows?

"I know we've had our history and I know we're like friends, and we're fine and all and-" He mumbled.

"Oh, spit it out Lucas." I prompted, knowing what he was going to say based on Carly and I's conversation a while ago.

"I *really* like her, El, like *really*. It makes my heart... burn? Feels good and awful at the same time." He sighed, finally tearing his eyes from her and directing them onto me, "Does that make it awkward?" He shot me a sad, sympathetic look.

I smiled at him, "Of course it doesn't, you guys are my best friends. Your happiness is my happiness." I slung my arm around his shoulder, a bashful smile covering his face.

My focus adjusted back on Carly who was finishing her speech, and running over to the both of us.

"You like my speech?" She danced over to us, bringing us both into a hug.

"Loved it." I smiled.

"You okay Luc?" She lifted his head up, pressing their foreheads together, his eyes immediately snapping out of their hazy gaze and completely focusing on her.

She pulled away, turning to face me but keeping Lucas wrapped in her arms, "By the *way,* I forgot to say, I ended up inviting Brady, a few of us wanted the day off tomorrow and he was wondering why and I basically ended up saying the more the merrier, I hope you don't mind." She batted her eyelashes with a sorry smile plastered on her lips.

I opened my mouth to react, but no words escaped, I immediately fell breathless.

I subconsciously began fiddling with the ring on my finger, "I'm just going to freshen up." I nodded, excusing myself to the bathroom.

. . .

I mmediately, I splashed my face with cold water, staring back at myself in the mirror. My head was invaded with a million thoughts, unintelligible. Thoughts of Brady and starting the new job he's given to me, and with Brady comes guilty conscience thoughts of Theo. A completely over-whelming sense of immorality and-

A harsh knock scared me out of my thoughts, a brash, "Hurry up!", startling me.

I quickly reapplied my lip gloss and made my way out, a body barging past me as soon as I opened the door and quickly slamming it in my face.

I scoffed, making my way back into the busy crowd, trying to find either Carly or Lucas, but bumping into a taller, stronger figure.

"I've been looking for you." His voice broke through the booming music, becoming the only sound I could hear.

I looked up, making intimidating eye contact with him towering over me.

"You're the only person I know properly here, I was about to start being awkward." He pulled me to the side, biting his lip.

"You? Awkward? I'll believe it when I see it." I laughed, thinking of nothing more ridiculous than Miles Brady being awkward.

"Okay, maybe not awkward, I just get nervous around new situations, I don't go to parties." He shrugged, offering me a sip of his drink.

I took it, swallowing it painfully and almost gagging at the taste, "God, what is that? It's awful." I smacked my lips trying to get rid of the taste.

He let out a throaty laugh, dipping his head, his hair falling

in front of his face, "It's scotch, assuming you're more of a sweet girl?" He licked his lips, a smile then breaking out.

"I guess so." I laughed, feeling my face grow hot.

I cleared my throat, trying to change the direction of the conversation, "I'm excited for tomorrow. To start the new job, I really appreciate you giving me the chance, Brady." I smiled.

"Let's not talk about work," He groaned, "Couldn't get out of it quicker."

"Okay, you want to dance instead?" I grabbed his hand in an attempt to pull him back into the crowd.

"I don't dance." He shot back the rest of his drink, effortlessly pulling me back towards him.

"It's either work talk, or dance." I folded my arms in front of me, his eyes flashing different emotions at me in the strobe lighting.

"Fine, let's dance."

He let me pull him into a crowd as he stood awkwardly, trying not to get pushed around as the drinks I had previously had caught up to me. I swayed my hips to the music, the lights slowly blurring into one another, the only figure I was able to focus on was the one directly in front of me.

I couldn't tell whether it was in my head or my alcohol blanket tricking me, but his eye contact felt so much more intimate, so much closer, the warmest I've ever felt it.

"Hey! You made it!" Carly sauntered over to us, waving her hands in the air, giving Brady a side hug and beginning to dance by my side.

"I'll get you both a drink." He cleared his throat, squeezing out of the crowd.

"Sooooo..." Carly nudged me playfully.

"Nooooo." I shut it down, "Let's not." I closed my eyes, pretending to shut her out by not seeing her.

"We'll talk about it eventually." She whisper-shouted into my ear.

"Of course, we will." I raised my eyebrows.

# Chapter Twenty-Two

## ELLIE

I was just finishing up the sauce and boiling the pasta when Maeve almost tackled me to the floor, jumping onto my side. I swung her around, landing her on my back and swaying around, making her feel like she was going to fall.

"Stop, stop, stop!" She giggled uncontrollably, gripping onto me for dear life.

I picked her up and put her on the counter, letting her catch her breath as she giggled in between breaths.

"I can't laugh anymore. I can't." She took a huge breath, flopping backwards so she was laying down on the counter.

I laughed at her dramatics and started getting the bowls out of the cupboard. I brought out 3 bowls, almost falling off of the stool I used to reach. I would say I'm pretty tall myself, I wouldn't say I'm short but a pretty good height overall. I would say that before I tried to get something out of Miles' kitchen cupboards because you would think he's 8 feet tall with how high his cupboards are.

"Ellie? Why don't you live with us?" Maeve chirped up again, "You work with Daddy all the time, and then you have play dates with me *all the time* so you should just live here. Plus! Daddy is *so* happy with you around, like obviously *I* make him happy but *you* make him happy like when he talks about Mummy, happy." She blurted out, very expressively.

I felt a sharp pang in my chest, never even hearing Brady talk about Maeve's mum, let alone Maeve actually bringing her up to me. My mouth ran dry, I turned to face her as she was fiddling with her fingers.

"Does he talk about Mummy a lot?" I started to slowly dish up her dinner, without wanting to pry too much.

"I guess. He says that he wants me to know her, even though I never met her." She extended her arms to me, gesturing to let her down from the kitchen counter.

I picked her up, putting her on the floor as she scampered out of my view to the other side of the living room. I watched her reappear in front of the draws by the TV, ruffling through the draw and pulling out a photo frame.

She skipped back over to me, handing me a beautiful golden frame with a black and white wedding photo of Brady and a beautiful woman with long brown hair pinned up into such an elegant bun.

"You look just like her." I crouched down, sitting cross-legged in front of Maeve, her hopping onto my lap.

"Huh... you do too." She tilted her head, looking between me and the photo inquisitively.

I smiled weakly at her before looking up at noticing Brady standing in the kitchen looking down at us. As weird as this sounds, the nickname Brady just suddenly...stopped fitting him. He seemed more deep, more real. He's not just my boss or my ex-boss, or some guy that I babysit for. He's Miles. He's had a meaning and a purpose in other's lives. He was a husband, he's a dad, he's Miles.

"Hi, Miles." I bit my tongue to hide my smile.

He looked slightly taken aback, the corner of his lip twitching, trying not to form into a smile, "Hi, Ellie." He nodded slowly, letting his lips curl up hesitantly.

We stared at each other for a moment, both breaking eye contact at the same time and looking to the floor.

"Not going to say hi to me?" Maeve hopped up from my lap, jumping into Miles' arms and sitting on his hip.

"What're you doing on the floor?" He chuckled, holding her up with one and reaching down to me with his free arm.

I took his hand, helping myself up, still carefully holding the photo frame in my hand.

I could feel the change in his demeanour as he noticed what I was holding. He quickly let go of my hand, clearing his throat and looking at Maeve with a quivering smile.

"Are you telling Ellie about your mum?" He squeezed her arm making her giggle slightly.

She nodded, snuggling into his shoulder. I gave Miles back the photo frame, smiling apologetically. He slowly took it from my grasp, admiring it for a second before propping it up on the kitchen counter, rather than placing it back into the draw.

"Dinner's ready." I cleared my throat, bursting the silence as I grabbed two of the bowls that I previously prepared.

Miles put Maeve down, giving her a bowl before she ran off to the sofa and made herself comfortable. He placed our bowls down side by side on the island, grabbing and giving me cutlery.

We sat comfortably in silence for a second before Maeve switched on *Tangled*, cuddled into her Max the Horse plushie, which was almost the entire length of her body.

I noticed Miles picking at his food with his fork, not actually eating any of it, with a look on his face indicating he was deep in thought.

"Everything okay?" I nudged his arm with mine.

"Oh, sorry, yeah, dinner's great. Thank you." He broke into a forced smile, nodded over-enthusiastically.

I paused before swallowing, "I'm sorry if I overstepped with Maeve and uh-"

"Amelia." He glanced over to the photo and then back to me, "You didn't, it's okay." He sighed.

"What happened? If you don't mind me asking, of course." I pried, not wanting to seem too desperate for an answer.

He cleared his throat, putting down his fork and completely facing me rather than sitting side by side, "She passed in childbirth. I remember the day like it was yesterday." I noticed tears beginning to well in his eyes, him managing to blink them back, "I'm sorry Sir, we've done everything we can, we're holding your daughter in the NICU, when you're ready." He recited.

I swallowed, trying not to make it obvious that tears were about to make their escape down my cheeks, "I'm so sorry Miles." I hugged him immediately, not really knowing how else my comfort could provide him with a source of aid.

I felt his arms wrap back around me, his chin resting on the top of my head and his whole body relaxed. As if he'd been holding in a breath this whole time, just for it to be released at that moment. We stayed, paused in a moment in time, waiting for the other to let go as if we both needed this.

He pulled away suddenly, as if he suddenly realised that he shouldn't be doing something. A cold draft entered between our grasp, him resuming eating his pasta.

"How's uh- Theo? Was it?" He prodded aggressively at the bowl; his tongue buried below his lip.

"Good, I think? He's in New York, and has been for almost 2 weeks. Haven't spoken to him in a couple days." I looked away from him, subconsciously fiddling with the ring on my finger, my focus suddenly shifted onto Theo.

We've been trying to get our relationship back to normal. Whatever normal is at this point. He left the day after our 'argument', promising that everything was okay and that we would facetime every day, which started off true. As of this week, his 2nd week there, he's been busier, with 'work and stuff'. Understandably.

"Are you still seeing each other? Like...dating?" He hesitated.

How on earth did he find that out? I don't recall telling him, nor do I-

Carly.

He most definitely asked Carly.

"No. We decided to just be friends." I exhaled.

"Mm. Okay." He nodded slowly, shoving a bunch of pasta into his mouth and turning his head away from me.

"Okay." I nodded back.

"Wis h y ou wer e h ere." He smiled, glitching halfway through his words.

"Miss you too Theo, how is everything going?" I questioned, propping him up against a book whilst making myself a cup of tea.

"G o od, go ing in to a mee ting now I c all y ou hour."

I sighed, knowing that it was absolutely hopeless trying to keep in good contact with him. For the first time, I actually felt guilty, upset that I wasn't there with him. If I wasn't so stubborn, if I was a better girlfriend...friend to him I would've just sucked it up and gone with him. But the past can't be changed and there's absolutely no use dwelling on it.

"Okay, talk to you-" I was interrupted by a harsh knock on the door, almost startling me enough to drop my phone. I hung up on Theo, knowing that he wouldn't hear my attempt to say goodbye anyway and trudged towards the front door reluctantly, not particularly wanting to see anyone.

I fiddled with the lock for a second before swinging the door open, my heart immediately surging in a happiness that I hadn't felt in a while.

# Chapter Twenty-Three

## ELLIE

"Theo?!" I gasped; the air struck from my lungs.

I jumped into his arms, not hesitating another second to feel his embrace again.

"What're you doing here? What- I've missed you so much." I pulled away, taking a look at his face, barely even trying to hide my smile.

"I've missed you too, Els." He placed a kiss on my cheek, a dimple popping out on either side of his face, "I thought I'd surprise you." He spoke as I pulled him inside, out of the cold and shut the door behind us both.

"Consider me surprised." I grinned, still holding onto his arm, as if he was going to re-slip out of my grasp at any given moment.

It's moments like these that scare me. Moments where I realise how much he means to me. Moments where I realise how much I miss when he isn't around and how much I value when he is. It's like a shield that goes over my eyes and he rips it right off whenever we're together.

He leant into me, hesitating for a second before exhaling

and leaning back. I took my hand off of his arm, taking a step back and realising how we left things before he left.

"So," I cleared my throat, "Tell me everything, I'll make you a hot drink." I hurried towards the kitchen, taking out a fresh batch of cookies from the fridge and placing two on a plate to heat up.

"It's amazing out there. Everything is going perfectly; we've finalised most of the contracts. I had a free week so I thought, why not come back and see my favourite girl?" He propped himself on the other side of the kitchen island, shooting me a cheeky smile.

"Your *favourite* girl?" I enunciated, over-emphasising my shocked glare.

"My only girl." He corrected himself, chuckling.

I slid the plate and a mug over to him, still shaking my head and laughing.

He cleared his throat, quickly, like he was trying to change the conversation, "Have you spoken to Olivia?" He quickly spoke up, spitting it out like he was waiting to get his words out.

"Uh- no, not for a while, why?" I questioned, curious as to why he suddenly brought her up. Not out of jealousy, of course.

"I saw her in New York. She mentioned you." His voice quietened, clearing his throat, again.

"Oh." I replied, not really knowing what to say.

"She came to get the last of her things from her house there. She's moving permanently to London." He continued, making the silence between each of our words slightly more and more intolerable.

"Oh, cool." I replied again, trying to sound slightly more interested than the last time.

He took a breath, about to continue his...ramble about Olivia? Before the door knocked.

I groaned, stomping over to the door again. I looked out the blinds of the window next to the door and my heart sped up...again.

What was he doing here? If Theo sees who's outside, he will go mental.

"Who is it?" He called, through a mouthful of cookie.

"Don't know yet!" I lied, yelling back to him.

I opened the door slightly, sliding out through the small gap and shutting it behind me, the cold immediately sending a chill down my spine.

"What're you- oh, hi sweetie!" I noticed Maeve hiding behind Miles' leg.

"Ellie!" She yelped, running towards and almost tackling me in a hug, "You didn't tell me we were having a playdate Daddy!" She jumped up in excitement.

*'I'm sorry'* He mimed to me, "I didn't know where else to go." He shook his head, looking down at Maeve.

"I know this is really inappropriate, you weren't answering your phone and I need to go into the city, I have no one else to call and-" He stressed, running his hands through his hair and down his neck.

Part of me wanted to calm him down, say it's all going to be okay, give him a hug and comfort him. Part of me wanted to send him away. I didn't want him to go into too much detail because of my own personal fear. Pathetic, I know. Since Theo left, the number of nightmares and cold sweats I've had have been ridiculous to say the least, but only one which I would consider a vision. The only difference being I didn't remember a single thing from that night. Not that I went wandering the streets, or driving recklessly into lamp posts but instead, I woke up and it was as if someone had wiped my memory. I didn't remember a thing. Naturally I didn't tell Miles because what would I say that wouldn't send him into a panic?

"Miles. It's your turn to breathe." I placed a hand on his shoulder, he chuckled, taking a deep breath, "I promise, it's okay."

"What's taking so long- oh." Theo appeared behind me.

I gasped, turning around with Maeve still by my side.

"Brady." He cleared his throat, sending daggers in my direction.

"Mr. Grey. Sorry for intruding." He nodded, flicking his gaze between me and Theo, confused.

"Just, call me when you're on your way back." I turned to face Miles again, giving him a weak smile as Maeve snaked her hand into mine.

"See you tonight, princess." Miles crouched down, placing a gentle kiss on Maeve's head, before standing up, smiling and heading back towards his car.

"What. The-"

"Language." I held my finger up to silence Theo's bad mouthing in front of Maeve, "Hey, honey, meet me in the living room, okay? We can watch Tangled." I ruffled her hair, as she squealed, clapping her hands and running off. I pulled Theo towards my bedroom, shutting the door behind us.

"What?" I sighed.

"You're joking, right?" His jaw dropped, "You've got the child of your old boss sitting in your living room and you're asking me what?" His eyebrows raised as he scoffed.

"It's not as weird as you're making it sound. Miles and I are friends." I shrugged, trying to reassure him.

"*Miles.* So, it's 'Miles' now?" He taunted, shaking his head.

"Oh my God." I muttered under my breath. He's reading *way* too much into this.

Of course, this isn't me saying that I feel absolutely nothing towards the man. This isn't me saying that Theo shouldn't be worried about him because that would just be misleading, and simply not true. But he can't be angry or upset with the fact that I'm helping him out.

"Fine. It's fine. Going to babysit my ex-girlfriends ex-boss' daughter. Casual."

"Don't say that, Theo. You've always been my best friend, why can't we keep it that way?" I felt a push against my heart at his words.

All these years and all he sees me as right now is his ex-girl-friend. It's as if the 20 years prior to the last couple of months means nothing to him. Like he got what he wanted out of me and now I'm useless to him.

"Yeah... yeah, alright." He sighed, walking out of my room towards where Maeve was sitting.

～～

"I don't get sugar rush. Please can I have one? Please?" Maeve clung onto my arm, shaking it slightly.

"You can ask your dad when he gets here, okay? It's late and you need to sleep." I carried her away from the cupcakes that we finished baking 10 minutes ago and got comfortable with her on the sofa.

"Ellie?" She spoke up after a few moments of silence, laying her head onto my lap, yawning.

"Mhm?" I stroked her hair out of her face gently.

"Can we have play dates all the time? I like being with you." She mumbled in between a yawn before she drifted off to sleep.

"We can have play dates all the time if you want." I whispered back, tears slightly welling in my eyes.

I watched the headlights pull up in front of my house, and

the sound of a car door opening, closing and footsteps coming towards the house.

I picked Maeve up, adjusting her on my hip while grabbing her coat and positioning it on her back, over her shoulders and opening the front door.

"Hey." Miles whispered, his eyes immediately settling on Maeve asleep in my arms, a smile growing on his face.

He looked exhausted, drained even. His hair was all dishevelled, his tie slightly loosened and his eyes dark, drained of all the colour and light which usually inhabits them.

"Do you want to come in?" I stepped aside so he could step in, out of the cold.

"No, thank you, I should get Maeve home." He held her back, allowing me to pass her over into his arms, "Thank you, Ellie, for tonight, for everything." He readjusted Maeve's coat on her shoulder and reached out, squeezing my shoulder.

"My pleasure, Miles, as always." I held his hand, resting on my arm.

He cleared his throat, his eyes darting towards where my hand held his, "On second thought, she'll be asleep either way, right?" He smiled.

I nodded, a smile subconsciously growing on my face as he stepped past me, heading back towards the living room.

"Do you want a drink or anything? I've got whiskey," I remembered the night at the bar, the vision of him downing his drink after our *moment*, "or hot chocolate, or tea or..." I continued remembering that he was driving.

"I'll just have water, thank you." He stood fiddling with his hands after putting Maeve back to lay down on the sofa.

He slowly walked over to where I stood in the kitchen, leaning against the counter, his eyes burning into me as I poured his drink.

"Is Theo still here?" I notice him looking around, taking in his surroundings.

"No, he went home a couple of hours ago." I shook my head, finally turning around and meeting his gaze.

He nodded, holding eye contact, and taking a few steps towards me, now towering over me.

"Here's your water." I gulped, holding out the glass to him, my hand uncontrollably, subtly shaking at the proximity I faced with him.

His scent immediately invaded me, disallowing anything but that, his gaze and his closeness to me to enter my mind. My mouth ran dry, my knees threatening to buckle underneath his presence.

"You're shaky. Are you nervous?" He took the glass from me and with his spare hand, brushed a stray strand of hair out of my face.

"You're- very close." I muttered out in one exhale.

"And are you okay with that, Ellie?" As if it was humanly possible to get any closer, he did.

I nodded, physically unable to get any more words out, anymore flustered than I was.

"Use your words, *Trouble*, I need to know if you're okay with what I'm about to do." He swallowed, his eyebrows pinch, his eyes frantically scanning my face, searching desperately for an answer.

What was he about to do? I found myself eager to find out, my body gravitating itself towards him. The thrill overrides the anxiety that his presence brings.

"Yeah- Yeah I'm okay with it." I managed to stumble over my words, breaking eye contact with him briefly.

He put the glass down on the counter beside us, now running his hand through my hair, down my chin, tilting my head up using two of his fingers.

"Look me in my eyes when you tell me that." The black of his pupils overtook his usually green eyes.

"I'm okay with it." I repeat myself, my head feeling light at the heat coming off of the two of us.

He wets his lips, his eyes glued onto my bottom one which I kept biting out of pure and utter nervousness. He ran his finger over it, releasing it from my teeth and pulling down slightly. His lips parted slightly alongside mine which he pulled apart. I could hear, *feel,* his breath get slightly heavier. We were that close that I could practically feel his heartbeat against mine.

He took a breath, leaning closer into me before a loud yawn startled us a few feet away from each other.

"Ellie?" Maeve mumbles from across the room.

Both of us take a step away from one another, finally able to breathe properly and redirect our attention to Maeve.

She sat up, moving so that she was now knelt facing us, "You're here!" She hops off the sofa, running and jumping into Miles' arms.

"Hey, Mae." He lowered his tone, rocking her back and forth, "Ready to go?"

She nodded into his shoulder giving me a tired smile and wave.

"Bye, Ellie." She yawned, almost immediately going back to sleep.

"Again, thanks for having her." He swallowed, making eye contact with me for the first time since... whatever that was.

"Yeah, no worries." My face flushed and I smiled at them both.

"Bye, Trouble." He looked me up and down before turning and heading for the door, leaving me frozen in place, stunned by what I had just experienced.

# Chapter Twenty-Four

## ELLIE

"Can you do me a favour?" I finally mustered up the courage to say to Miles who had been sitting across the room for the last few hours.

It's almost been a week since our little *moment* in my kitchen, and not that it's been awkward or anything, but he's been so much more open and upfront, and flirty to say the least. In a weird way, it's been more comfortable around him. I feel like there's less of a need to have a wall up around him, or act a certain way.

"Of course I can." He said without ceasing typing or looking up from his laptop.

"It's been on my mind for a little while and I just don't know where to start, it's stressing me out and I just need to start somewhere and get it over and done with and-"

"Breathe. What do you need?" He sat up, closing his laptop and moving next to me.

"I need you to look into my family. I know you aren't meant to do this but just on the database, I need to know about them, anything they've done or I don't know, just anything."

"Okay." He agreed, a lot more easily than I thought it would be.

"Okay? That's it? No remarks or disagreements?" My jaw hung slightly open.

"Of course not. Anything you want." He got up, "I'll print off whatever I find." He started heading to his office to access the database.

"Thank you!" I called after him, a smile immediately spreading but dropping on my face.

This was too easy. Now I actually have to find out about my family. I'll actually be reading information about my ancestors and this could give me all the answers to everything I've questioned in the last couple of months. The paper Miles prints off could explain everything about my visions and the craziness that goes on in my head. Or. It could explain nothing. And I'll be left hopeless, at the beginning, all over again.

My heart raced; my mind was no longer able to settle on the few emails that Miles set me to send. The time ticked louder and louder as the minutes passed, waiting for him to stumble back out of his office with a sheet of paper in his hand, or absolutely nothing.

"Okay. I found some stuff." He sped out of his office, taking a seat next to me with a staple stack of papers in his lap.

"Oh my God." My jaw dropped at the amount of 'stuff' he found. I turned to face him, not knowing where to start, not knowing how to feel or react to this situation, "Oh my God." I repeated, shaking my head.

"I didn't read anything, just in case." He handed me half the stack.

"Okay...okay, you read that bit, I'll start on this." I nodded slowly, trying to comprehend my entire family history suddenly placed into my lap.

I skimmed over the first couple of pages, talking about my mum and her drugs, her NA meetings, brushed past my dad and his registry in the marines and then settled on something that I had never even heard before.

*Henry Moore – deceased*
*Cause of Death: Domestic murder*
*Rose Moore arrested and sentenced to life in prison.*

I took a deep breath, not knowing who they were, knowing they were my family and feeling a pang of guilt, heartbreak, regret – for God knows why. I skipped through a couple of pages and *that* is when it got weird.

*Edward Moore – deceased*
*Cause of Death: Domestic murder*
*Penelope Moore arrested and sentenced to life in prison.*

"When were these murders?" I pointed them out to Miles, curious as to when they started.

"I have them too, back until..." He paused, flicking through the pages, the list of names getting longer and longer each time, "1898. It's a bloodline thing. Every first-born daughter has killed their partner, or in 'mysterious circumstances' since 1868." His face ran pale, him clearing his throat and exhaling slowly.

"*Fuck...*" was all I could mutter out. My stomach churned at the thought of whatever godforsaken curse that my family has on us, "So you're telling me, my family is the reason...I'm crazy?" I tried to dissect the information that he's given me.

"It's weird. It's like some sort of curse." He mumbled under his breath, barely loud enough for me to hear, "I don't believe in curses but this?" He pointed, still shuffling through the pages, "It's *weird,* Ellie."

"There has to be some sort of logical explanation, right?" Tears pricked my eyes, my breaths becoming scattered.

I stood up, letting my history fall to the floor, pacing in front of Miles.

"Ellie." Miles stood up, cutting off my pacing.

"Miles." I tried to say something but it was as if someone had stolen my voice because nothing came out, nothing but shallow breaths and panic.

"Breathe." His voice reached into my soul.

"I can't." My lungs refused to let any air in, my brain went into complete overdrive, trying to understand what I had just learnt, "There's no escaping this. There's no getting away or getting free or being *fucking* stable at all. That's it. That's just who I am. I'm meant to be absolutely, criminally insane. I'm just insane." I threw my hands up, tears now streaming down my cheeks subconsciously.

Without saying another word, I was embraced into Miles' arms, pressed against his chest. His heartbeat echoed into my ear, bringing me back down from my cloud of anxiety and grounding me into his grasp. I breathed in a strong whiff of his cologne, making my head spin slightly.

I snaked my arms around his waist, pulling him tighter into me, holding on for dear sanity. He clearly didn't mind the patch of tears which were slowly soaking through his shirt, or my unstoppable trembles, which he just squeezed me tighter when they came around more aggressively.

"You are so much more than *just insane.*" He said the words like it disgusted him.

He pulled my head up from his chest so we were now making eye contact. He swiped his thumbs underneath my eyes, his expression softening into a sympathetic glance, "So. Much. More. And you don't even know it."

I took a minute to soak in his words before pulling away and finally being able to breathe. It was like he attached himself to me and I was immediately relaxed, able to breathe, able to think, able to function without spiralling. He completely calmed me, reassured me.

"I'm-"

"Don't you dare apologise. This would freak me out too." He flashed a small, tight-lipped smile at me, before guiding me to sit back down, "I'll order us some food, I can look further into this, you just...relax."

I sighed, relaxing into the sofa and pulling a blanket on top of me. The house settled into silence and he pottered away into the kitchen.

"When is Maeve coming back?" I yawned, appreciating the calm vibe with just the two of us.

"Her grandma," He cleared his throat, "Amelia's mum, is going to drop her back here later."

I nodded, making a mental note to myself to try and leave by then, to avoid the awkwardness.

"She was upset when she found out that you were going to be here and she wasn't." He chuckled, making his way back to me with two hot chocolates, setting them down on the coffee table, "She also made me promise to make you a hot chocolate. Apparently, they're the best in the world." He sat down, running his hands down his lap.

"Thank you." I smiled, sitting up and taking the warm mug into my hands, immediately sending a chill through my body.

.   .   .

The sound of a knock at the door startled me awake, only now realising that I fell asleep. *Shit.* How long had I been asleep for? And why didn't Miles wake me up?

I stayed as still as possible, remembering that Miles' mother-in-law was dropping off Maeve 'later'. And if this was her, I was asleep for a solid 2 hours. There is no way.

All I remember was ordering and eating our food, deciding to watch a movie, and Miles lit the fire while he was still looking through paperwork about the Moore side of my family and... nothing. That must've been when I dropped off.

"Goodbye honey!" A woman's voice called from the door as I heard the sound of small footsteps running down the hallway, "How are you, Miles?" Her tone changed to quite an empathetic tone.

"I'm fine thank you, Betty, thank you for having Maeve today." He spoke quietly, obviously trying to keep his voice down.

"My pleasure as always, darling." There was a brief silence, broken by her clearing her throat and stepping inside, "Maeve kept mentioning someone called Ellie today." She stated in an attempt to pry for more information, "Are you seeing someone?"

It felt wrong to just lay here, eavesdropping, and as much as this could be the worst, most irrational decision I've ever made, I decided to sit up, stretching and yawning, pretending I just woke up.

I turned to face the door, feigning shock as I laid eyes on the woman standing by the front door. She had bright blue eyes and her curly, greyish blonde hair was hung down by her shoulders.

"I'm so sorry, I didn't realise anyone was here." I got up, rushing over to shake her hand.

She seemed slightly stunned, really looking at me. *Really* looking, head to toe, scanning my face over and over again.

Miles stepped in, noticing her shock, "Ellie, this is my mother-in-law, Betty." He gestured towards her.

"It's a pleasure. Forgive my shock, you just look like...like" Her eyes welled up as she got slightly snivelly.

"Maeve told me the same." I smiled, laughing slightly to ease the tension I felt building.

She brought me into a tight hug, my body freezing in shock. I looked over to Miles over her shoulder and he just shrugged, showing a slightly concerned look.

"Sorry, darling." She pulled herself away, composing herself, "Same time next week?" She nodded enthusiastically, turning to face Miles.

"Same time next week. Thanks again, Betty." He nodded slowly, shutting the door behind her as she left.

He turned to face me, immediately reading my facial expression, "Don't be mad that I didn't wake you up, okay? You were clearly tired and needed to sleep." He shook his head, laughing.

"That was the most awkward interaction ever. You could've woken me up before you answered the door at least!" I nudged his shoulder, laughing slightly and trying to maintain my annoyance at him.

Before I knew it, Maeve came sprinting down the hallway, catapulting herself into my arms and screaming, "Ellie!"

"I've not gotten a greeting like that in years." Miles huffed, turning his back on us.

Maeve tugged his shirt bringing him closer and he spun round, placing an arm round me and also on her back, giving her a gentle kiss on the forehead.

"How was Grandma's?" He spoke, pulling away as I put her down on the floor.

"It was good. We drew pictures and I drew this." She hopped over to the door, grabbing her *Frozen* Elsa and Anna backpack and taking out a colourful sketch.

"This is you Daddy, that's me. That's Mummy and that's Ellie." She pointed to each individual person, Miles being extraordinarily tall, Amelia drawn with a halo and wings around her, and me with a huge grin and what looks like a cookie in my hand.

"What's that in your hand?" Miles pointed out a yellow square scribble that she'd included.

"The photo in the frame of you and Mummy, duh!" She rolled her eyes as if that was obvious.

I looked up at Miles, seeing tears brimming his eyes as he quickly tried to blink them away, wiping his cheek as soon as he noticed me staring.

"Come, Maeve, let's put it on the fridge." I held out my hand and she quickly took it, skipping towards the fridge without hesitation.

I picked Maeve up so she was high enough to adjust the magnets on the fridge, alongside a few other drawings that were dated over the last few years. I noticed Miles speed out of the room, from the corner of my eye, down the hallway, and heard his office door shut in the distance.

"Perfect!" Maeve chirped up, admiring her work.

"I'll be right back, okay?" I put her back down, letting her wander off and do her own thing, following Miles down the hallway.

"Miles?" I called out for him meekly.

I stood outside his office door, not knowing if I should make the step to see if he's okay, but before I let my brain talk me out of it, my hand was there, knocking on the door.

"Come in." His voice croaked from behind the door.

I peered in, noticing Miles sat on the floor with his elbows resting on his knees and his head in his hands.

As I came in, shutting the door behind me, he looked up, my heart immediately shattering at the sight.

His eyes were puffy, his hair all tousled from where he'd obviously been running his hands through it. His lips were tucked in between his teeth, and he was visibly taking deep breaths trying to calm himself down.

"Oh, Miles." I immediately became teary-eyed, simply seeing him in a state like this, knowing he was that hurt, that upset, but was okay with me seeing it.

The second I made my way over to him, kneeling in between his legs and taking his head into my hands, a few tears slipped down his cheeks, one after another, and another, and another.

"I, I miss her. So much, Ellie. I can't." He took frantic breaths in between each word, eventually letting his body weight sink into my arms in sobs. His head cradled into my shoulder, gripping my body like it was his last remaining source of air on earth.

His body shuddered, pulsed under my arms, the most I was able to do was caress his back and his head.

"I'm so sorry. I'm so sorry Miles." Was all I could think of to say, holding his head into my chest.

"I thought it would get better. And, and it never does." He gasped, now ceaselessly crying into me, grasping any air he could from around us.

I bit my lip, struggling not to descend into tears myself.

We sat in silence, broken occasionally by his tremors of cries.

# Chapter Twenty-Five

## ELLIE

"I don't want you to leave on a bad note. What's wrong?" I sat down, slinging my legs over Theo's lap and handing him his mug of tea.

"It's stupid. Really." He tilted his head against the back of the sofa and sighed deeply.

"It's not stupid if it's bothering you." I ran my hand up and down his shoulder, trying to comfort him in any sort of way.

"It *is* stupid if I'm playing jealous boyfriend when I'm not even your boyfriend." He rolled his head to the side, now giving me a hopeless look.

I sighed, pressing my lips together. Deep down I knew this was going to be about my relationship with Miles. It's never about anything else, "What do you want me to do?"

"Will you hate me if I say that I don't want you to see him as much?" He pouted, frowning slightly.

A knot formed in my throat, my heartbeat speeding up and my stomach dropping. The thought of not being able to see the one person who unconditionally supports me, crushes me. But, if it comes down to being supported by Miles, or have Theo in my life? I can't lose my best friend. I'd rather go another 20 years without knowing what true understanding and support feels like, than lose Theo.

"I work with him, T." I said, confusedly.

"But you also babysit for him, you spend a lot of time at his house in general and, I don't know. I told you it's stupid." He groaned.

"No, no, you're right. It's okay. I won't see him outside of work, I promise." I agreed, reluctantly, part of me already wanting to break that promise.

I woke up to the sound of what seemed like my front door creaking open, which is...weird, because it doesn't usually creak. Heavy footsteps echoed through my hall, seemingly getting closer and further away at the same time. The comfort and warmth of my duvet tucked around me no longer felt comforting, nor warm. It felt empty, cold, suffocating. The sound, a muffled monotone voice, repeating itself in rhythm with its steps. It was as if it was going on forever, invading me rather than confronting me, coming from every direction, inside my head, outside my door, occupying my home. Until it came to a stop outside of my bedroom door. The shadow looming under the small crack in between the door and the floor. I could just about make out the shuffling of two feet, the shadow, too threatening for me to look too hard.

I could feel my every heartbeat resonate into my throat, shaking through my hands, the duvet now covering my mouth to forbid any sort of fear to escape.

The door slowly opened, allowing a stream of light to enter and slowly overtake the darkness of my room. Except the light that entered was anything but light. It was murky, eerie, ghostly almost.

The shadow loomed in my doorframe, anticipating my movement to finally take the leap through the darkness. With my every quickening breath, its footsteps glided towards me, its presence becoming increasingly more intimidating by the step.

Within a blink, the darkness had moved on top of me, invading me, restricting my breath completely. Its physical presence now impending on me, disallowing for the darkness to just go away, to just fade into light. Nothingness. My breath still restricted, clawing at me for some kind of escape out of my inevitable suffocation. I could hear a voice, *her* voice, laughing at my demise. Laughing at my end, *the* end. Until the end was suddenly a lot closer than I thought it would be. Ripping me from the invaded comfort of my own home into the abyss of my mind, slamming me right back down and startling me awake.

The air suddenly flooded back into me, like it was getting pumped into my body. My head ached just as if I had been flung around the room, hitting every corner possible. My eyes focused on the room around me, regaining consciousness, the sick feeling immediately surfacing and threatening to leave my body.

I heaved myself up, immediately coming to contact with the body already sat up in front of me, previously touching my forehead.

"Hey, hey, hey. You're okay." Theo whispered, placing his lips against my forehead, "You were moving a lot, cold sweat too." He added.

I took a breath, finally settling into my surroundings, finally realising I was safe, "God." I sighed.

"Nightmare? Or uh- vision?" He stuttered, breaking eye contact with me.

"Something like that." I cleared my throat in an attempt to get a coherent sentence out of my mouth and failing.

"You sounded quite urgent when you scheduled today's session, are you okay?" Dr. Taylor smiled at me.

"Everything's fine. I was just...putting off seeing you again, and I knew I would have to face it eventually and, I don't know." I shrugged.

I hadn't come to therapy in quite a while, knowing that I was putting it further off, the more chaos that entered my life. Everything with my family, the ups and downs of everything with Theo, and *everything* with Miles. There's no good place to start the explanation, nor somewhere to stop it.

"I need some advice." I started, "Family wise."

"That's exactly what I'm here for." She put her notebook down, pulling her chair towards me.

"We've obviously talked about my family before, and family history and my visions and... everything about that. Well, you were right." I sighed, "We don't exactly know what or how but there's been history in my family, some dodgy, weird, creepy stuff, and I still need to look into it more but I'm trying. Actually trying to understand it." I smiled, knowing that I wouldn't care anywhere near this much a few months ago, finally seeing some progress in myself.

"That's amazing Ellie. If you don't mind me picking up on something...'we'?" She tilted her head.

I cleared my throat, "Miles. He's been helping me a lot, and supporting me, he encourages me...in everything and I just feel really...safe around him, I guess." I shrugged, breaking eye contact.

"I'm glad you can voice that about him, it seems like you feel safe enough to not only open up to him, but to me about him too. Again, if you don't mind, how is everything with Theo?" she picked up her notebook, flicking back through the previous pages.

"We decided to just be friends." I nodded, the guilt entering my system all over again.

"How do you feel about that?"

"Okay, I think? I see so much potential in Theo, but he's my best friend, and I can't lose him. I can't. He's playing jealous boyfriend when we aren't even together anymore and he's told me to stop seeing Miles as much and I stupidly agreed because I'm so scared to lose him because Miles is always so supportive and he's never judgy and he's just...everything." I sighed deeply, not knowing I needed to get that off my chest, "I can't have both, but I can't choose either. I can't lose either of them but, I don't know. It's hard."

"I'm going to go on a tangent here, and give you some advice not as your therapist, but as someone who has been in a similar position that you have. Pick the person who helps you grow, who makes you feel like your best self. Someone who makes your soul shine and your heart glow. Who you can smile unconditionally with, whilst still having moments which can heal you. You can't force yourself away from someone who your soul is meant to be with, no matter who you don't want to lose." She took a breath whilst smiling, as if she was reliving some of her own memories.

Her words repeated itself in my head. That is exactly what I needed to hear and I didn't even know it. I felt a new, refreshing wave wash over me. As if I'd been in a trance this whole time and her words wiped the slate clean, clearing and refreshing my vision and thoughts.

"So, you think I should choose Miles?" I asked, suddenly even more confused than I was before.

"If that's who you think about when I told you that, I think you have your answer." She smiled.

# *Chapter Twenty-Six*

## ELLIE

*ook who I found.*
    *Look. Who. I. Found.*
    She sent me a photo, captioned *look who I found*.

Of course, Olivia and Theo just *had* to be in New York at the same time, taking pictures of them kissing each other on the cheek, getting coffees, getting cute little yellow taxis together, times square and whatever amazing things you can do in New York. I'm not jealous at all. In fact, I quite literally told Theo that I would rather stay here in London than travel all that way anyway.

She just didn't need to rub in my face that they're seeing each other. Actively. On purpose.

The admittance of my jealousy kicked in, and not because they're spending time together or because they want to see each other. Simply because the ring on my finger, promised myself to him, and *obviously* something happened between them, whether that was while Theo and I were together. I don't know. Part of me wants to be furious that for 20 years, all he's preached is his love for me, and how amazingly he would treat me, and to give him a chance. I give him that chance and he breaks my trust, he's practically chosen her. Maybe he threw himself straight in the deep end and was struggling to tread water, maybe he was genuinely just unexpectant on what he was going to have to deal with with me, or maybe he just didn't know what he was getting into. But the second he got what he wanted, he threw it away, he immediately drifted away. Of course, that's not all his fault, but can a girl just channel her pain and regrettable jealousy into him for once?

I immediately got into my car, putting my foot down and driving as if there was no end to the road. My unknown destination. My every destination.

I knocked on the door. Knocking...and knocking...and...

The door flung open, the weight of my knock almost making me fall into his house.

"Hey Trouble," he smiled, "Are you okay?" He dropped into his serious expression from a playful smile.

"No." I walked past him, throwing my phone onto the sofa and pacing around his kitchen, "It's just so. Frustrating. I can't! I can't with him anymore. He has to be doing this to wind me up. Come on!" I paced, making grand gestures with my hands and running my hands through my hair.

Miles took a seat next to where I was pacing back and forth, his eyes following me back and forth.

"Ellie?" He spoke up.

"God! It's like I mean nothing to him, I express my feelings and he just proves he can move on in like, what, a week?" I groaned.

"Ellie." I noticed him stand up, blocking my path of pacing.

"Miles, you have to understand me, right? I'm not being crazy."

171

"You're not being crazy. Now take a breath." He took a deep breath, gesturing for me to do the same, "And explain what's happened from the top." He guided me towards the sofa, sitting me down.

I inhaled deeply, ready to explain the whole situation, "Theo's gone back to New York, and just conveniently, our childhood friend Olivia has recently come back into the picture who even more conveniently is *also* in between New York and London, who so obviously still has somewhat of a thing for even though he claims he's so focused on me and so in love with me. It's always going to be her at the end of the day, I mean, who would've thought? It was all Ellie this and Ellie that until he had Ellie and now it's Olivia this and Olivia that." I groaned, "She is exactly to me what you are to him!"

"What does that mean?" He looked puzzled by my finishing statement.

"He asked me to stay away from you... because he didn't-doesn't like how close we were- are. Truthfully, he asked me to stop seeing you outside of work, and I would never do that to him- I just- he can't be my jealous boyfriend when he isn't even my boyfriend!" I said, getting angrier by the minute.

"Do you want me to be honest with you?" He placed a hand on my thigh, turning me to completely face him and shuffled closer to me.

I nodded, making solid eye contact with him.

"Theo *never* deserved you." He whispered, almost as if he was scared to see how I would react.

His voice, his words immediately settled my anger, tears pricking the back of my eyes. Why does he have to say absolutely everything right?

A silence settled around us, only leaving the subtle crackle of the fireplace echoing throughout the house. Leaving us soaking in each other's presence, waiting for one of us to make the inevitable next move.

His hand glided up my thigh, now holding my waist, pulling me closer to him, his eyes settling onto my lips.

His hand warmed my cheek, slowly pulling me closer, allowing my brain to run a million miles a minute, allowing my heart to work overtime.

That inevitable moment when our lips collided. It was so much more than I imagined it to be. The passion, the warmth, the comfort. The safety and the support. Everything he makes me feel physically embodied into our kiss. It was like swimming through fire. Except the burn was enjoyable, I would never want this to end. As slowly as this happens, our lips moving through one another's as if we had all the time in the world to waste, my heart couldn't be pounding any faster.

It'd be a sin not to kiss him again, and again. And again.

He pulled away, my lips following, yearning for more, eventually separating us. Our breaths filling the silence. His hand staying on my waist, our eyes closed, simply just taking in the pure and utter bliss of a moment.

I felt his smile against mine before I even saw it with my eyes. That smile, that would just be too cruel not to kiss.

"You have a way of making me feel at peace, so calm and...I hate it." I whispered onto his lips, rewarding a chuckle from him.

He shook his head, pulling away from me slightly and finally looking into my eyes, making my heart surge harder than I ever thought possible.

"You...it's just you. I have no words." He stuttered trying to find the right words to match the feeling that we just shared. Finding it seemingly impossible.

He kissed me again, pressing our lips together more forcefully, less cautious and more passionate. Cupping my cheek and pulling us impossibly closer together. I felt myself wanting, needing more, needing to constantly have his touch on my skin, and his words against my lips. I've never felt so calm yet somehow set completely on fire. Every hair on my body stood up, a chill wavering completely over me, opening my eyes yet also keeping them closed.

I pulled away, trying to catch my breath, our breathing through each other no longer fuelling my oxygen but only growing the fire inside of me.

His hands stayed on my cheeks, our foreheads remaining together, our eyes heavily fixated on one another.

"That was a bad idea, you know." I pulled my head away from his, adjusting myself and laying my head on his lap, looking directly up at him.

"Why?" His smile flickered, not knowing where I was going with this.

"Because..." I paused, embracing the comfort that I felt in his presence, his hand running through my hair, "Now that we've kissed once, there's no reason for us not to again." I felt my cheeks warm.

"And, that's an issue...why?" His eyes wavered over my face.

"It's not." I smiled, turning onto my side, watching the fire flicker in the fireplace, allowing us to just live in the present for once.

The least I could do for accidentally sleeping over here was make breakfast. Right? That's a completely normal, friendly, houseguest, friend, just friendly thing to do. Right? Right.

I saw a small head of brown hair bob along the bottom of the counter, appearing next to me with a beaming smile on her face.

"Pancakes?" She squealed, gesturing for me to pick her up.

I picked her up, letting her sit on my hip, using my free hand to keep an eye on the bacon sizzling in the pan.

"And bacon!" She wiggled in my arms out of pure excitement.

"Good morning to you too, Maeve."

"Best. Morning. Ever." She bounced as I placed her on the surface next to where I was cooking, "Can you stay over every day? Daddy doesn't make good pancakes and I can just *tell* you do." She inhaled dramatically, taking in a good whiff on the aroma.

Just as I was about to give her a grateful response, Miles strolled into the room, yawning and ruffling his hand through his hair.

My eyes glazed over his half-exposed body, his red and black chequered trousers sitting low on his hips and his torso so perfectly-

"Looks- smells delicious." He spoke, walking over and leaning against the counter next to Maeve, "Morning, pumpkin. Morning, Ellie." He said with a sultry smile on his face, kissing Maeve on the forehead and hugging me from behind.

My words failed to greet him, leaving him hanging with an amused look plastered in his expression and his chin resting on his shoulder.


After breakfast, I decided to make some cookies before I left, subconsciously putting off the moment I actually had to leave. I would stay in this atmosphere forever if I could. The warmth, comfort, support. A life away from the chaos, away from the craziness of every day. Some peace.

My wrist started to cramp up from the speed I was trying to mix this batter. Why on earth does Miles have this 'special flour' that gets tough so quickly? Gluten free flour shouldn't be something that exists. Controversial but baked goods without sugar and gluten? Baked bads. Simple as.

I groaned exaggeratedly, dropping the whisk into the bowl and running my hands over my face, undoubtedly getting flour everywhere.

"What's wrong?" Miles chuckled from the sofa on the other side of the room.

"The cookie dough is way too tough, there's no way these will taste good." I sighed, leaning against the counter and turning to face him.

He started to make his way over to me, stopping briefly at his record player, sifting through multiple vinyl records before pulling one carefully out of the stack.

He set it up and *My Girl* by *The Temptations* started to play, the sound immediately soothing me and easing the tension chilling through me.

I turned back towards the dry dough sitting in the bowl, alongside the 10 eggs that I've failed at cracking, alongside the spilt milk and sugar everywhere.

"Maybe it's just not a baking day today." Tears pooled in my eyes; a lot more emotional than I should be over failed cookies. I sniffled, leaning on the counter and holding my head in my hands.

"Hey, it's just cookies, it's okay." Miles came up behind me, snaking his arms around my waist, pulling me up against his chest and swaying slowly, "No use crying over spilt milk, huh?" He joked, pointing to the milk all over the counter. I chuckled through sniffles, reluctantly, leaning the back of my head against his shoulder.

He hummed along, singing some of the lyrics and occasionally going back to humming *'my girl, talking 'bout my girl...I've got sunshine on a cloudy day'* placing kisses on my cheek in between each lyric.

"This may sound really sudden, but this is really what I've needed, Ellie. This is really what I want." His voice was soft, serene, still swaying along to the music but spinning me to face him, "You're home to me."

"Me too, Miles. This feels like home for me too."

# Chapter Twenty-Seven

## ELLIE

Staring into his eyes gives me the exact same feeling every single time I do, from the moment we first kissed 3 weeks ago, to every kiss, hug, smile, touch since then.

We're sat on my sofa, simply just taking in each other's presence, a frequent routine for us.

As much as I feel awful for kind of doing this behind Theo's back, since I *did* promise not to see Miles outside of work, but considering the way he makes me feel and the fact that Theo's been in America for weeks and weeks on end, he can't expect me to sit and stay here alone every day. We aren't dating and he can't be mad at me for...moving on?

"Do you want anything?" He said, slipping our hands out from each other and walking over to my kitchen and grabbing two mugs, already knowing my answer without me having to reply.

"I *want* you to come back over here. I was comfortable." I fake-sulked, turning on my music on the TV for some background noise.

He chuckled, working his magic on our hot chocolates

before bringing them over to where I was sitting and leaving them on the coffee table. He knelt on the sofa, slowly making his way over to me and propping himself up either side of me, our faces a few inches away from each other.

"Hi." I smiled, pushing myself up to kiss him.

"Hi." He whispered back, leaning down and placing a kiss on my nose, then either cheek and finally settling on my lips.

I untucked my arms from underneath him and slunk them around his neck, pulling him in closer.

He dropped his arms, now interlinking them behind my back and laying on top of me. I could feel his shallow breathing, just as he could most likely hear the exhilaration dancing through my heartbeats.

"Can I ask you a question?" I hesitated, knowing that this topic would just keep repeating in my mind until I inevitably worked up the courage to ask, "It's kind of personal."

He sighed, propping his head up on my stomach to look at me, "Let me guess, is it about Amelia?" He tilted his head to the side.

"How'd you know?" I brushed a hand through his hair.

"To be honest, I've been waiting for you to ask since Maeve brought her up and obviously since...uh," He swallowed, breaking eye contact with me, probably thinking about the time that I found him upset in his office.

"We don't have to talk about it, I was just... curious." I say, realising how awful I must sound, "What was she like?"

He turned his head to the side, sighing, "She was, everything. It was like she was heaven sent. Just when I needed her, she came right into my life like an angel on earth and just... completely turned me around. I didn't want kids, I didn't even believe in love and now, she's the reason I have the most precious thing in my life. It's like she knew she wasn't staying long and so she left me with a constant reminder of...her. I can't describe it; she was just simply perfect in every way." He paused, "Sorry, you probably didn't even want that much detail." He shook his head.

"No," I moved his head to face me, giving him a small smile, "I want to hear everything you have to say. And more."

He nodded. I could tell this was a long time coming, something he needed to get off his chest so all I could do was simply listen.

"All these years, since she's gone, I've been so isolated, so focused on doing right by her and doing right by Maeve, and nothing else, I almost tricked myself into thinking that she would hate me for moving on, or even just trying to." He took a deep breath, "I forgot that was exactly what she wanted. She had her time with me and gave me Maeve, just to hold on to the hope and love and just pure ecstasy that she brought into my life, and naturally, when she passed, I forgot all of that." His head tilted back in my direction, "Until I met you. When Prescott first hired you, everything about you reminded me of her and I was so cold and distant because I was scared to put myself through that again, I wasn't ready to move on. Amelia will *always* have my heart, I do believe she was my first true love and of course she's Maeve's mother, and I will *always* love her." He put emphasis on his words, almost as if he really wanted me to hear them, "Ellie, you've taken a place in my heart that I didn't think anyone would hold ever again and that's terrifying to me." His voice trailed off towards the end.

I inhaled, trying to search for the right words to respond, not knowing remotely where to begin.

He must've sensed my hesitation because almost immediately after my sigh he sat up, "You don't have to say anything. I just want you to know that this is it for me. I really care about you and I really really do like you Ellie." He grabbed my hands, pulling me up from laying down and pulling me onto his lap.

"It's not that I don't want to say anything, I just don't know what to say. It's just you." I repeated his words to me, to him, giving him a gentle kiss.

We held eye contact for a while, really just *connecting* with each other, a smile tempting both of our lips.

"You must be joking." A voice cleared from my front door, a set of keys dropping to the floor.

I pulled away from Miles, my heart catapulting at the scare I just had.

"Theo!" My mouth ran dry, a knot forming in my throat.

I slowly stood up, leaving Miles sat on the edge on the sofa, Theo's expression disgusted, flicking between Miles and I.

He scoffed, shaking his head, rubbing his eyes as if he were trying to get himself out of a nightmare, "You must be joking." He repeated.

"Theo, please listen, hear me out." I walked slowly towards him, careful of what I could possibly say that could set him off.

"Hear you out?" He laughed, throwing his head back in amusement, "Hear you out." He crouched over, trying to conceal his laughter before stopping abruptly and making his way over to Miles.

He grabbed the collars of his shirt, pulling him up towards him and spitting in his face.

"Theo, Jesus!" I pulled him away from Miles, standing in between them with an arm's length distance separating us.

Miles stood back up, his jaw tensed, his fists clenched, attempting to make his way back over to Theo but my hand against his chest stopped him.

"Do you not care about me at all? About us?" His expression was cold, belittling, condescending.

"Of course, I care about us, I just- I'm not in love with you Theo. I can't wait for you to decide whether you want to be with me or whether you want to work on us, I just- can't do

181

this possessive, jealousy, relationship non relationship thing." I sighed, turning to face him.

"You're always trying to make me look like the bad guy." He rolled his eyes "I try to do something for us and somehow it still gets spat back in my face. All I've done for the last 20 years is *try. For you.*"

"I'm not blaming you for anything, and I can't take the blame for not loving you Theo, we're meant to be friends." I emphasised my words, "Just. Friends."

"I have always loved, appreciated, needed you *so* much more than you need me and you *know* it."

That's not true. That's not true and he knows it. I would probably be homeless, dead somewhere without him and he knows it. He's just trying to throw his anger back in my face, which is fair, because it is my fault, I shouldn't have promised him that I wouldn't see Miles. I wanted to scream back that it wasn't true. I wanted to yell at him that I need him more than he ever knows but my words wouldn't allow me to speak. I was frozen, physically, mentally, emotionally, and the only thing bursting my heart into flames was his finger repeatedly prodding against my chest.

"*You* are the problem. This would've worked if you *tried*. God, this is insane, I knew this wasn't going to work. You should've just stuck to your guts and shut me down again."

"How is that my fault? You wanted me to shut you down again after *years* and *years* of asking me to be yours but it's not good enough when I slip up and make a mistake? You're meant to be my best friend T; we're meant to be best friends. You knew it would change. You knew it would be different if we dated and look at where it's gotten us!" I shoved my full force against him, creating some distance between us.

"Don't play the victim here Els. Don't do it." He gritted his teeth and shook his head at me.

"If you so much as say another word." Miles groaned, rolling his eyes, pulling me to his side.

"This doesn't concern you." Theo took a step towards Miles, squaring up to him.

"It concerns me when you hurt Ellie. And clearly..." Miles started, gesturing to me, directing Theo's attention to me. Tears pooled in my eyes, a shake shivering over me.

"Man, Els, why didn't you just say you were whipped in the first place?" He let out a hearty cackle, slapping his knee sarcastically, "Could've fooled me while we were together."

"Whipped, you're hilarious." Miles nodded, plastering a grin on his face and patting Theo's arm.

"Are you really going to stand here and tell me you were loyal to me? The whole time?" I stepped in front of Miles, practically begging Theo to tell me the truth, "God, I mean, I saw the way you talked about Olivia, even how she talks about you and the way you were posed in New York together, come on!"

"Don't turn this on me." He shook his head.

"Admit it." I shoved my finger against his chest.

"Yeah, okay. We slept together. I slept with Olivia while you were off with Brady. We're equal now."

"No. No, no, no we aren't. I was loyal to you right until the end. You wanted this. You started this and you were the one who begged so *desperately* for this and you go on and ruin it? Make this make sense to me, please!" I held his arm, begging for some sort of explanation for his behaviour.

"You want an explanation. Have you ever thought that maybe just *maybe* I didn't want to feel like some pity date for you? I know you; you got sick of me asking and you just said yes because at least I'd get out of your hair."

"That's not true." I interrupted him.

"Now you have Mr. Miles Brady. So, let's just settle our

differences and call it a day." He spat out, anger practically bubbling out of him.

Without another word, I separated myself from the closing gap between the two of them, walking over towards my dining table where I had left something of Theo's. Something that once was the most important thing to us both.

I grabbed his hand, forcing the ring into his palm and closing his fingers over it, "Give that to Olivia." I scoffed, "And please. *Please,* get out." I managed to spit out without bursting into tears, "And leave your spare keys on the side, you won't need them anymore." I choked, taking a few steps back before hitting brushing against Miles who was still standing behind me.

"You're okay." He whispered to me as Theo left, slamming the front door behind him. He held me as I fell back against him, breaking into a fit of sobs, my entire body convulsing, "You're okay."

# Chapter Twenty-Eight

## ELLIE

"I found this." Miles dropped onto the sofa next to me, handing me a thick book.

*The Psyche by Julia Walter-Moore.*

"Moore...as in..." I looked at him in shock.

"Mhm. She's your great grandmother, way way back." He flicked through the folder that rested on his lap, "It's about predictions. From the tiniest of things like finding money on the street, to births and deaths and drastic life altering events. She also talks about the past having a direct link to the future, fixing your past means fixing the future." He turned to a certain page, showing me the quote that he'd read out.

"So, you think there's a chance this is all happening because there's something... unresolved... in my past?" I sighed.

"Possibly." He ran his hands through his hair.

We'd been at this for 3 hours, it's understandably tiring chasing the same lead for hours on end not knowing when you're going to get somewhere.

"Do you have any family you think you could talk to? Who might know anything about this?"

"I haven't talked to my dad in- in like, 10 years. Think I should start there." I sighed, holding my head in my hands.

The thing is with our relationship, there was no absolute reason why it faded. I went off to university and it just... died out. I didn't want to associate with my mother, and my dad was a constant reminder of her and everything I was put through in such a short amount of time, so teenage me thought, 'why not start fresh?' and that's exactly what she did. The worst thing about it all? He didn't even try to reach out to me.

My leg bounced aggressively under the table; my lip pinched in between my fingers in an attempt to settle the nerves which were stirring up every emotion in my body. I couldn't keep my vision locked on one thing for more than a second, my eyes darting in every and any direction possible. Until they finally settled on a man, looking just as nervous as I was, taking in his surroundings and then settling his gaze on me.

I couldn't quite make out his expression. Hints of worry, fear, regret; flashes of love and confusion and nervousness all mixed into one.

I stood up as he approached my table, both of us standing idle in front of each other, not knowing what to do, not knowing what to say.

"I'm sorry." He apologised immediately, taking a step towards me and reaching out his hands.

I took a step back simultaneously, stumbling over my chair slightly, "Dad, please, I-I don't really know what to say." I took a seat, him doing the same opposite me.

"I'm sorry that I didn't reach out, I left you all alone when you needed me. I'm sorry." He teared up, "I've missed you awfully and- I was overjoyed when you reached out, I- uh, how did you find me?"

"I have my sources." I smiled slightly thinking of how easily Miles tracked him down, forcing myself to get on track with the conversation, "Dad, I need to ask you a couple things, it's really important, okay?" I leant forward trying to keep my voice down.

He nodded enthusiastically, "Of course, anything."

I took a deep breath, knowing I would just sound absolutely insane if he didn't know what I was talking about, "Has anyone, ever, in the family, had- like…visions?" I stuttered out.

His eyes widened, his mouth opening slightly.

I ruffled through my bag, bringing out the book and sliding it towards him, "This is mum's great grandma, right?"

He sighed, taking a deep breath and swallowing, "I had a feeling that this is why you contacted me." He chuckled under his breath.

"You knew?" A shaky breath exhaled from me.

"Your mother warned me about this when she was pregnant with you. She said it runs in the family and there's nothing we could do to avoid it. And when I left… she couldn't take it, that's why…"

"You left because of me? So, you're-you're the reason we were always alone and-and the reason why mum started drugs and drinking and *basically* why she killed herself?" My heart tightened in my chest, restricting my breath and forcing tears out of my eyes.

"Sweetheart, you have to understand where I'm coming from. Your great grandmother used to have visions, on visions, on visions, and when they started to come true, everyone neglected her because they thought she was just… insane. Same with your mum, and when she learnt that the drink and the drugs would stop the visions, she went for it."

"You left me." I suddenly became so much more upset about the situation than I ever was. I always used to convince myself that I didn't care, or that I was just simply better off without, and clearly that's just simply not true. Clearly it was just buried feelings.

We sat in silence, composing myself, and finally realising what he said.

She drank, she did drugs, she did all of this just to stop the visions. *I would kill for them to stop.* Maybe she was right. Maybe I hated her all this time for something that was just completely out of her control.

"It's hereditary." I whispered.

"Yeah." He softly agreed, "Listen El. There's been a lot of murders, and well, murderers in our family. You need to stay safe."

"I *am* safe. I promise."

I stood up, preparing myself to leave. I didn't realise how overwhelming such a small encounter could possibly be, "Anyone else I need to know about?" I partially joked, knowing everything I needed to know, *for now.*

"Actually, Ellie." He started.

My heart dropped into my stomach, my feet forcing me to walk away before I could hear another word. There isn't any more that I need to know. There *can't* be any more.

I felt my head spin as soon as the air hit my face. I felt my eyes going hazy, like my consciousness was whipped out of my soul, like my head was about to explode. I couldn't keep myself from swaying back and forth before I couldn't control anything at all.

It was as if I blinked myself into another realm, the second I reopened my eyes a black figure appeared mere inches in front of my face. I could feel her presence, smiling, taunting me right in front of me but so far beyond my reach. She'd never been this close before.

"Oh, Ellie, Ellie, Ellie. What am I going to do with you?" a ghostlike eerie whisper echoed through me, the world surrounding us morphing, people suddenly appearing in every direction, spinning, running, laughing, screaming.

The hooded black figure warped into a small girl, standing hesitantly, expectantly in front of me with an orange bucket in her hand.

"Trick?" She glared at me, her eyes burning into mine.

I stared right back at her, not knowing where to take this encounter.

"Or trick?" she tilted her head to the side, a smirk crawling onto her face.

I shook my head, not understanding. Halloween was right around the corner; all the days were blending into one but surely this is just a weird coincidence?

She repeated herself, over and over again, her face becoming more and more distorted, her voice becoming deeper and rougher with each breath as she grew much taller than me, eventually towering over me, taking the rest of the world with her, until it was just her darkness.

I could barely stay attached to myself, my soul drifting further and further away from my physicality, simply unable to hold on any longer.

# Chapter Twenty-Nine

## ELLIE

"Wake up! Ellie, Ellie, Ellie! Come on, please wake up!" I felt a pressure bouncing on top of me, my eyes adjusting from the darkness recognising the body on top of me, "Daddy, she's awake!" Maeve screamed excitedly, "Happy halloweeeeeen!" She waved her hands above her head, making ghostly noises.

"What?" I croaked, groggily, still in a hazy confusion as to where I was and how I got here.

"Hey, you alright?" Miles came into my vision, sitting beside me and placing a cold towel on my forehead, sending a shock into my body.

"How-where, How'd I get here?" I whisper-shouted, shooting to sit up.

"Mae, I'll meet you in your room okay, go get ready for a bath." He gave her a kiss on the forehead as she nodded and ran off.

He adjusted himself, snaking an arm around my back and helping me sit up properly.

"I got concerned when you didn't come back after lunch

with your dad yesterday so I went to the restaurant and they had you in their medical room, they said you passed out right outside."

My mouth went dry at his words, my brain suddenly choosing to remember yesterday's events, "And- and now what? Where's my dad?" I panicked, knowing I ran from him when he needed to tell me something, wondering if he saw the whole thing.

Miles sighed, taking a glance behind him and shooting me a nervous look.

"No. He's not here- Miles don't tell me-"

"I'm sorry. I didn't know what to do. He begged me to let him see you again." He brushed a hair out of my face.

My dad stepped into my field of vision, holding his hands together in a praying motion, "Ellie, you need to listen to me."

"No." I tried to stand up, the blood immediately rushing to my head and making me fall back down again.

Miles caught me in his arms, rubbing his hand against my back, "I'll leave you two to talk." He went to stand up but I stopped him.

"Please, stay." I held his hand tight, pulling him back onto the sofa.

He nodded, resting his hand on my thigh and relaxing against the sofa, whilst I stayed on the edge of my seat.

"Your visions...how...bad, are they?" he avoided eye contact like he would catch the plague if he looked at me.

"Murders. Really gruesome murders. And they come true!" I smiled, getting tired of explaining this to people.

My dad pressed his lips together, closing his eyes and running a hand through his hair, "This is worse than I thought." He cleared his throat trying to cover up.

"What's that meant to mean?" Miles and I spoke up simultaneously, looking at each other and showing a smile.

He exhaled deeply, sitting down next to me, "Listen. When you were younger, your cousin and you had a *really* close and special bond. You were inseparable. You guys would spend every blinking moment together to the point it was almost as if you had a twin mindset. You'd speak at the same time, the same things, we were all convinced you could read each other's minds. One day, your mother came to me saying that you were talking all sorts of gibberish, saying things like 'Macy wants to come over to play' and we would get a call from your aunt Willow saying Macy wanted to come over. It was weird to say the least." He finally met my eye contact, "Macy went missing while you were both still young, yet you *still* had somewhat of communication with her, until it just stopped. You told us everything and we found Macy's body a year later."

My heart sank. It was as if I formed a bond and it broke all within the space of his explanation. The only question is why do I have absolutely no memory of her? Maybe this was the feeling that I was missing. I was always aware that I didn't know everything, that there was something off, about my past, something I didn't remember. And she's it. Suddenly I feel like my past has been completed again.

"That's not all, when you turned 16, and Willow got into an accident, it's because she was driving to see me, because you started saying things again, dangerous things, about Macy. It was like she was still alive. Telling you to do things like a devil on your shoulder. Willow tried to look into it and there was just absolutely nothing. When Willow died and you and I lost contact, it just...fizzled. I kept track of you to see if anything would happen, like dangerous or crazy, but nothing."

"But it's started again. All my visions... is it her telling me her plans...of murder?" I felt bile rise in my throat, "But you said you found her body?"

"The police found her body. Willow couldn't- she wouldn't confirm." He admitted defeatedly.

"Oh." I exhaled deeply, turning back to face Miles, trying to seek any sort of comfort from him but not even that working.

I stood up, unlinking my hand from Miles' and my arm from my dad's. I hobbled over to the kitchen sink, splashing cold water onto my face and trying to breath, and failing. My heart rate speeding up the more I thought about it.

"Ellie." Both Miles and my dad stood up at the same time, the room starting to spin all over again, their voices echoing and repeating over again.

I leant my head on the kitchen counter, praying that closing my eyes will make this all go away, "Please, please, please, please, just go away. Please leave." I mumbled through sobs, muffled by my arms covering my face.

Arms enveloped me, a warm embrace settling my shakes, "I don't know what to say." Miles' voice murmured from behind me.

"Neither do I." I took a breath, moving into his arms and hugging him back.

***

"You have to." Miles dragged me up off of the sofa where I've resided since my dad left this morning.

"No, I don't want to." I sulked, groaning and pulling myself up reluctantly.

"Come on, Ellie, it's *just* trick or treating. Look how excited she is." Miles whispered, gesturing to Maeve bouncing around whilst simultaneously struggling to get the rest of her costume on, "What're you afraid of?" He nudged my shoulder, teasing me with a sultry smile on his face.

"The dark...?" I lied, "I don't know, okay? People. Murderers."

"It's a kid's holiday, where we'll go house to house asking for sweets or chocolate. I'll be right there, and so will Miss... whatever she's dressing up as." Miles looked between us, confused.

"Hey Mae?" I called out as she turned to face me quickly with her arms stuck in her t-shirt, sticking up in the air, "What...are you?" I crouched down to her height, helping her out.

"I'm Daddy! Can't you tell?" She pointed to the red and white striped tie which knotted loosely around her neck.

I burst into laughter immediately as I heard Miles' sigh, "You're meant to be something scary, sweetheart." He shook his head, chuckling slightly.

"Well, Ellie told me *ages* ago that you were a scary man, so." She shrugged, tugging on her oversized trousers.

My jaw dropped open as I tried to stifle the giggles which kept leaving me.

"Maeve! You were meant to keep that between us." I laughed, recalling our earlier conversation, bringing her into a tight hug and looking over my shoulder at Miles' amused expression.

"You think I'm scary?" He whispered into my ear as Maeve trotted off towards her bedroom.

"No. I *thought* you were scary. You know, back when you were actually my boss, before you became a softie." I tapped him on the chest, shooting him a taunting smile.

"I can still be scary." He gasped dramatically.

I gave him a surprised look, trying my best not to give in to his tempting gaze. He stalked towards me, grabbing and picking me up in one effortless swoop, throwing me on the sofa and trapping me in between his legs. He grabbed my wrists, smiling down at me.

"I'm so sorry, officer, what're you arresting me for?" I leant up, placing a gentle kiss on his lips.

"Theft, many cases of it." He shook his head with a sarcastic frown plastered onto his lips.

"Theft? Really?" My jaw dropped open.

"Mhm. Stolen my heart right in front of my eyes." He sniffled, pretending to cry.

I scoffed, "You're so corny." I sat up, kissing him again and swivelling myself off of the chair, "I'll come trick or treating on one condition. You have to dress up too."

"Trick or Treat!" Maeve screamed at the top of her lungs and held out her pumpkin bucket expectantly.

"Having fun yet?" Miles nudged me on the shoulder.

"Sure." I laughed, shaking my head at him.

"You fit right in, don't you worry, Trouble." He chuckled, referencing the devil horns I bought last minute out of pure fear that I would look like the boring one.

That was until we decided on what costume he'd be though. Of course, with Maeve being Miles, the only right solution was that Miles would be Maeve. Maeve braided a singular plait into the middle of his hair, sticking out of the top of his head with some light makeup from Maeve's flip phone makeup kit and his nails painted a shiny, sparkly pink.

"I don't think it's fair that you refused to wear the tutu. You've failed your costume." I shook my head at him.

I rolled my eyes, laughing and plastering a smile on my face as the door opened to-

"Marnie?" My jaw dropped open, just as her smile flickered, as if unsure whether to smile or not.

"Ellie!" She prolonged my name, her eyes widening and flicking between Miles, Maeve and I. She cleared her throat, looking down to Maeve and noticing her still waiting for her treat.

"Here you go, cuteness." She dropped a few sweet packets into Maeve's basket and smiled.

Just as Maeve was about to say 'thank you', a scary mask popped out from behind Marnie, crouching down and yelling. Maeve jumped back, screaming, hiding behind Miles' leg before rolling her eyes resulting in a nervous chuckle from Marnie.

The man whipped off his mask through a deep laugh, suddenly stopping when he laid his eyes on me.

"Ellie." He bit his lip, looking at me expressionless and slowly nodded his head.

"We should go." I cleared my throat, grabbing Maeve's hand and starting to pull her away from Theo and Marnie standing at the door dumbfounded. I felt Miles' hand brush the arch of my back as we walked away stiffly.

"That was the worst encounter I've ever had." I mumbled, slapping myself on the forehead.

"We could've avoided their house if you told me where they lived, Ellie." Miles groaned through chuckles, equally as awkward.

"I haven't been to their house since I was a teen and I'm pretty sure they've moved. They *definitely* didn't live that close." I sighed.

"It's fine, at least one of us is happy with that house." He pointed at Maeve skipping along the road a couple paces ahead of us.

# Chapter Thirty

ELLIE

I haven't gone home since Theo and I's argument out of pure fear that he might turn up and pick a fight again, and I just simply do not have that in me to fight against him. In the nicest way possible, it feels much less disrespectful that I'm staying with Miles now that Theo actually knows about whatever it is we have going on. When he didn't know, I still felt like there was some sort of element of cheating, even though we weren't even together.

Theo has this awful way of making me feel guilty for seeing other people even when he's made it clear that he has, or maybe it's just my subconscious telling me what it thinks I want to hear. I don't know what I want to hear. I know, I *know.* I'm also screaming at myself that Miles is the only right option. I don't know what it is, I just can't let Theo go. He's done so much for me and as much as I should hate him right now, it's hard to let something go that you've held onto for your whole life.

I shook my head, shaking the thoughts of Theo out of my head and cuddling into Miles' arm, pulling the blanket over my shoulder.

"Are you okay?" He whispered, craning his head and looking down at me.

"Mhm, just thinking." I sighed.

"About?" He sat up, pulling me up with me and turning us to face each other.

"Theo." I mumbled under my breath. This man could practically read my mind, there was no use lying to him.

"About your argument?"

I nodded, "I don't know Miles. It's just, he's really hurt me, and I can understand why he's hurt because of me too. I just don't want to lose him, is it bad that I don't hate him? Am I being stupid? Like, am I giving him what he wants by feeling guilt for being with you?" My words flew out at the end not realising where I was going with my sentence.

I inhaled sharply, not knowing how he would react or if he would lash out at me for being unsure about our... relationship?

"No, you aren't stupid, Ellie. Theo's been your best friend for basically your entire life, it's understandable." A wave of relief washed over me at his reaction, "I don't want you to feel guilty for what we're doing, I know I enjoy it and I hope you do too... fully." He tucked a loose strand of hair behind my ear.

"What *are* we doing?" I looked up at him, giving him the most hopeful look I possibly could.

Miles opened his mouth to start talking, before a loud three bangs echoed through the house from the front door.

"*Jesus.* It's probably just Betty." He unravelled our hands, getting up and opening the door.

I laid back down, getting comfortable again before I heard what sounded like Miles getting slammed against the wall and a gruff, "Where is she? I know she's here."

I shot up in my seat, spinning my head towards the door and immediately rushing over, "Theo, stop!" I yelled, pulling him off of Miles and shoving him away from us, "What're you doing here?"

"Why haven't you been home in *days*?" He slurred, clearly on something.

"You've been at my house?" I scoffed, shaking my head.

"I need to talk to you. Why haven't you been home in days?"

"You're the one that came storming in saying I'm the problem and telling me to just shut you down again." I rolled my eyes, crossing my arms.

"I'm sorry. I didn't mean it. I know I'm a jealous piece of shit I just can't control it when it comes to you." He sighed, tears pooling in his eyes.

"Go home, Theo." I grabbed his arm firmly, him stumbling and his weight falling onto me.

"Can we talk later? Can you come over? I promise I'll stop bugging you after." He stood outside the door, leant hazily on the doorframe.

I bit my lip, feeling Miles' gaze burn into me, almost daring me to say yes.

"I'll talk to you later." I muttered out, pushing him away from the door and shutting it in his face.

Miles scoffed loudly, shaking his head at me, his shirt slightly crumpled from where Theo had grabbed him, "You know what, I change my answer. I don't- I don't get it. Help me understand why you give him unlimited chances." he followed me back over to the sofa.

"Can you help me find something about that book? I forgot to ask." I cleared my throat, trying to change the subject.

"Don't change the subject." He sat down next to me.

"I'm not, I just forgot to ask. Think you left the paperwork in your office." I tried to get him off my back.

"Jesus, Ellie." He rolled his eyes, "Just answer the question."

"I- can't." I exhaled slowly.

"Yes, you can. I know you know why you do it." He pushed.

"Miles, please."

"Ellie."

"Come on-"

"I'm not leaving this alone anymore."

"God. Fine! You want to know why so badly? Because Theo is the only constant that I've ever had in my life despite how overbearing and overprotective and jealous and possessive he can be, he's the only person who truly knows me. Inside out. He always shows up. He always gives me a chance. He is always *there*. With or without our fights and arguments he's always there." I huffed out in one breath, panting by the end of it.

Miles' expression softened, the darkness leaving his eyes, "Let me know you, inside out." He took a step towards me, grabbing my hands, "You know you have me, always. Let yourself have me." He whispered.

"I only have you because you want to unpick my brain, you think I'm crazy." I sniffled, giving into his warm touch.

"I don't think you're crazy. I think you're a lot of things; funny, caring, you have an amazing personality, you're beautiful, but you aren't crazy." He leant forward, touching our foreheads together.

A rapid buzzing of my phone interrupted our moment.

I swallowed, pulling away reluctantly and checking my phone, looking up at Miles who looked equally as disappointed.

With no surprise, I clicked on what felt like the million messages from Theo. Harmless threats telling me that we need to talk *or else.* That I should come over and chat to sort things out *or else...or else...or else.*

I rolled my eyes, "I need to go and talk to Theo. I'm sorry." I gave him a quick hug, not allowing myself to see his probably disappointed expression.

"Ellie." He called just as I reached the door.

I avoided turning around to greet his eye contact, keeping my hand on the door handle.

I heard him sigh a few times before tutting a few times, "Nothing. Nothing. Just, text if you need anything." He muttered under his breath.

I nodded, hesitating to leave before deciding I should hurry up and get it over with before I changed my mind.

# Chapter Thirty-One

## ELLIE

" I know I screwed up. I know. Just please let me make it up to you." He pleaded in front of me, "You know that I don't mean what I say when I get angry, I know it's a bad habit but you make me want to change. You know this." He grabbed my hands, staring into my eyes.

I stayed quiet for a bit, truly settling into the realisation, trying to count the number of chances I've already given him.

"You're going back to New York soon anyway, are you not? Why does it matter if we're okay or not." I shook my head, tired of the constant back and forth between us, "Plus," I paused, not knowing whether it was the right idea to continue but deciding to anyway, "When you go out there, you'll have Olivia." I shrugged, pulling my hands out of his grasp.

"I thought we were over this." He groaned.

"We haven't talked since we fought, Theo, how do you expect me to be over it?" I scoffed.

He took a deep breath, "We *can* be over this. We can work on ourselves, and we can be better than ever." He followed me towards the sofa, sitting down next to me.

"You admitted to me that you slept with Olivia, while we were together, and you want me to jump back into a relationship with you like nothing happened? Yeah, we weren't suited in *that* way but it still hurts, T?!"

"At least I admitted it to you." He shook his head.

"What is that supposed to mean?" I sighed, flopping back onto the sofa, running my hands over my face.

"You slept with Miles while I was away. I won't be mad at you; you can tell me." He turned to face me, shooting a patronising smile.

"Oh, come on. Just because you made a mistake in our relationship, doesn't mean you can push it onto me." I groaned over-exaggeratedly and stood up, looking down at him, "Let's be honest, you would be furious if I did sleep with Miles, even though I haven't even blinked twice at the fact that you were with Olivia, may I just *reiterate* we were still together? Again?"

"I get that you're angry, I just-"

"But you don't get it. You really don't. It's like- all these years you've wanted me and now that you have me... I mean nothing to you." Anger and sadness merged into one, bubbling out of me, unable to stop myself from spitting and spilling my emotions into my words.

He sighed, hesitating for a second, "I don't want to fight anymore. That's all we've been doing recently. I'm sorry, really."

"We didn't argue for 20 years, it was bound to happen eventually." I mumbled.

A silence dawned upon us, sitting in one another's realisation for a while, "I'll be who you need me to be. As supportive as you need, whenever you need to listen or anything. From this moment forth. Promise." He smiled weakly, mumbling under his breath.

"Okay. Okay, fine." I reluctantly gave into him, completely unbothered to fight anymore.

"Start over?" He suggested, reaching out his hand to me.

I took it, trying to fight the smile on my face, having my best friend back, not having to worry about him breathing down my neck when it comes to Miles, or anything else for that matter, "I'm Ellie. Nice to meet you." I said, taking 'starting over' to a whole new level.

"I'm Theo, it's a pleasure." He smiled, his dimples pinching his cheek, the way I've always loved about him.

"Let's go out, I mean- let me take you out. All my treat." He grinned.

"Fine." I rolled my eyes, laughing.

We walked under an arch, mesmerised by the turtles, and little fishes swimming all around us in the glowing blue light.

"That one kind of looks like you," I joked, trying to find and pointing to a funny looking fish.

"Me?" His jaw dropped as he held his chest dramatically, "He clearly has *your* eyes."

We shared a laugh, sighing simultaneously and exchanging eye contact, "This is nice." He sighed, looking at me gleefully.

"I've missed this. Us, just existing together, happily." I smiled. He linked his arm around my shoulder, resting his head on top of mine.

"I've missed this too. I'm sorry I ever tarnished this. I took what I had for granted and that's no excuse for my behaviour, but it's not fair on you."

"It's okay, it's in the past." I smiled up at him, "Just... don't do it again and we can move on," I shrugged, taking a few steps towards the tank, laughing.

"Yes ma'am." He placed his hands on both my shoulders, leaning his head on my shoulder.

We sat on a bench, watching people walk by. Young, old, families, individuals, everyone leading different lives yet in the exact same moment as each other.

"What do you think they're doing here?" Theo pointed to a man, a woman and 3 children.

"I think...family day out, she's going to be their new step-mum and the two little ones are overjoyed but the eldest is *not* happy." I acknowledged the teenager falling a few feet behind them, on her phone with a sour expression on her face.

"Gasp! That's shocking." His hand flew to his mouth, making an exaggerated gasping noise, "To top it all off, she's in a fight with her boyfriend that no one knows about, she's not allowed to date until she's 18 but her birthdays in two weeks so it's fine." He shrugged.

"Plot twist, they've been together for a year. How can you keep a secret for that long? Honestly admirable." I chuckled, shaking my head, "Okay, okay, now them." I nudged Theo to look in the direction of a boy and a girl on the other side of the fish tank, seemingly screaming at each other, but muffled by the glass.

"Defo brother and sister, see! Look at that, he just shoved her and stuck his tongue out. That's sibling behaviour." He cackled, the sound bouncing off the walls and sending a chill down my spine.

A muffled 'I'm gonna kill you' followed by the pair storming off made us both throw our heads back in laughter, quickly followed by an older couple following them, rolling their eyes.

We settled our laughter, sighing in harmony and smiling at one another.

# Chapter Thirty-Two

## ELLIE

My hearing was muffled, everything surrounding me dimmed but also so much clearer than usual. A hazy blue waved around me, a floating...swimming sensation suddenly enveloping me. It was as if I had anchors dragging me to the ocean floor, the water filling my lungs, flooding me, drowning me. The feeling of water engulfing the little air I had left, my body convulsing as the water around me blurred into a black oblivion.

I sprung up, the supposed water still bubbling in my throat, choking me, leaving me gasping for air.

A gush of air finally filled my lungs, just as quickly as I realised the reason why I was snapped out of my dream so quickly.

My phone rang aggressively on my bedside table, my eyes unable to tell who was calling, still slightly blurred and hazy.

"Hello?" *His* voice echoed from the other line. My reality immediately snapped back into me.

"Hi... Miles." My voice croaked, a feeling of guilt immediately washing over me from not reaching out to him since I left his house the other day.

"Are you okay? What's been going on, I feel like you've been kind of distant since you left mine."

"No. I mean- yes, I'm fine, I'm sorry, I just-" I sighed, not having any excuse for why I haven't reached out, giving him a million different mixed signals, "I'm sorry, I can't talk right now, Speak later." I coughed out.

"Ellie-" he started, before I reluctantly hung up the phone.

I groaned, falling back onto my bed and yelling into my pillow, muffling it.

"Els?" Theo's voice made me jump up, scaring me.

"Hi, morning." I sighed.

He came and sat next to me, a suspicious smile plastered on his face, "I thought we could go on a little road trip today. Stay for the weekend, just to get away from the city, you know?" he suggested, smiling, with a hand making its way to my leg.

"What about New York? When are you meant to go back?" I yawned, still adjusting to everything that's happened in the 2 minutes I've been awake.

"I'm not going back. At least not for now. I really want to work on us, I mean it, and if that means staying here, so be it." He explained.

I really appreciate his gesture, but the guilt for dropping Miles for Theo all of a sudden is swallowing me. I feel like a horrible person just dancing and hopping between them both, but it's not on purpose. Part of me will always hold onto how Theo has treated me, how on and off he is with me and how Miles is always just 'on'. Always what I need, always supportive, always perfect in every way.

Almost as if he heard my thoughts he spoke up, "I want to be here for you. I want to be all you need."

I nodded, brushing past what he said, "Well, are you going

to let me get dressed?" I got up, pulling him towards my bedroom door and shoving him out.

"20 minutes!" He called through the door.

"I feel like we haven't properly caught up in ages, tell me everything." He said, one hand on the wheel, glancing over to me.

I sighed, realising how much he doesn't know and wondering where to start, "Long story short, my visions keep getting worse, I found out it was a biological thing and my mum's side of the family is, well, basically insane, I spoke to my dad and he told me I had some insane connection with my cousin and so now we think that she's the one killing people and telling me her plans about it, but they all thought she was dead but surprise, it was never actually her because my aunt didn't want to confirm it, and honestly? Now that I'm saying this again is kind of making me freak out because I haven't actually sat down and thought about this in ages, I've just been distracted and busy and now... yeah, now I'm freaking out." I took a deep breath, my voice getting caught in my throat.

The car came to a stop at a red light, Theo shooting me a horrified, confused look with his jaw hung slightly open, "I don't know what to say." He shook his head, stunned, "I'm sorry I've not been here for you." We started driving again in silence.

My heartbeat in my ears silenced any other words that Theo was saying, the world speeding by outside, making me feel dizzy, and a churning suddenly surging through my stomach.

I closed my eyes, taking a deep breath, feeling Theo's hand

grab mine, sending a wave of comfort through me, bringing me back to the ground.

"How's work going? Is everyone treating you right? Oh! Who was that man you came with on Halloween?" Marnie sat me down as soon as we walked into their beach house, talking my ear off with questions.

"He's- uh, a friend, him and his daughter, yeah." I stumbled out.

"She was doing her boss a favour." Theo came up behind me, handing both me and his mum a hot chocolate, not the best one in the world, for sure.

I nodded, remaining quiet, also giving myself a mental reminder to talk to Miles after this weekend.

"She wasn't stressing you out too much, huh, babe?" Theo hugged me from behind, causing me to recoil out of his touch slightly.

Marnie gasped, covering her mouth and squealing, "Oh, it's finally happening, my favourite son and my favourite girl are finally together?" tears brewed in her eyes.

"I'm your only son, ma." Theo chuckled.

My mouth hung open, my words failing to correct Marnie's wrong assumption, quickly glancing to and from Theo, expecting him to correct her but, obviously not.

"Can we talk outside?" I whispered to him, plastering a fake, stern grin on my while tugging his arm.

"Yeah." He nodded quickly, pushing me in front of him to walk, grabbing both our coats, hats and scarves on the way out.

. . .

I stood by the ocean, watching each individual wave roll in and out, remembering the feeling of what it felt like to drown, over and over again. The thought simply making me dizzy.

I reached down, feeling the water, the shock of how freezing it was stunning me back into reality.

Taking a few steps back, I subconsciously bumped into Theo, turning around and looking up at him, giving him a disapproving look, "Why did you let her believe we're dating?" We remained in quite close proximity.

"Because I couldn't bring myself to tell them how much of a piece of shit, I've been to you." He fiddled through his pocket, slowly bringing out *the* ring.

"No." I shook my head, tears brimming my eyes, "I don't want it."

"Please." His voice broke, the sound breaking my heart.

He took his free hand, holding my cheek and pulling our foreheads together.

"You really hurt me; you know." I frowned, his hand against my cheek catching the tears slipping out.

"I know, sweetheart, I know. I'm sorry."

"And you know that I'll forgive you every single time. It's not fair, Theo." I leant into his grasp.

"I know." He whispered.

"Because, I love you. I do. Maybe not in the way you want me to, but I do." I sniffled.

"I love you too. In all ways. I let my jealousy and just ignorance towards you and everything you're going through get in the way and I'm sorry. I'll tell her we aren't dating; I just want us to be completely okay again."

We both nodded, taking a breath in sync.

# Chapter Thirty-Three

## ELLIE

" I don't even see why this is a choice. Brady helps you, supports you without asking, you love his daughter and him clearly and he's good for you. I don't even want to count how many times you told me Theo apologised in that story." Carly groaned, giving me a confused look after I just completely laid onto her everything that has gone on in my life, filling her in on every word, every action, every conversation with Miles, Theo, my dad, the visions. I'm surprised she didn't have a heart attack, taking it in all at once. Yet now, obviously, we're onto the romantic choice part of the conversation.

"He's my best friend Carly. I can't just ditch him, I can't."

"And you're mine, and as your best *girl* friend, I can't let you keep forgiving him. What would you say to me if Lucas called me whipped, over some other guy?"

I sighed, rolling my eyes, "I would tell you to leave him." I admitted reluctantly, "*But,* we aren't together! And he's apologised!"

"Apology shmology, doesn't matter." She banged her hands on the table, attracting shocked looks from the people sitting around us, "Mi amorcito, I love you. Theo is not good for you. And that's not me saying pick Miles, I'm telling you to pick yourself."

I nodded, knowing deep down that she was right, coming to terms, for the millionth time, that I am better off without Theo. Looking back I'm happier, I'm less stressed, I'm less on edge. But he's my best friend. He's been around forever and part of me has always known that he always will be around, even through all of our blips and arguments and fights.

"I can't be with Miles if I'm working on my relationship with Theo. It just won't work." I shrugged, trying not to be bothered by that, but knowing this decision is hurting more than any other I've made before.

"So, you aren't going to see him again." Theo reinstated for the fifth time.

"That's what I said, yes." I cleared my throat, searching frantically through my bedroom drawers, "Theo, have you seen that picture box you got me for my birthday? I can't find it anywhere." I threw piles of clothes over my shoulder, messing up my orderly piles.

"No, I haven't. What do you need it for?" He opened my wardrobe, helping me look, "Who's is this?" He picked up Miles' hoodie, his expression feigning confusion.

"Oh, it's mine. Decided to shop in the men's section for once." I exhaled a nervous laugh, snatching the hoodie from him and quickly tying it around my waist.

For my therapy session today, Dr. Taylor has told me to bring items which represent the people who have made impacts on my life. People who I care about and who have recently impacted my life. Miles' hoodie, Theo's photo box. I pulled out my old memory box from underneath my bed, slowly pulling out a photo frame of my dad and I, wrapping it in some tissue paper and shoving it in my bag.

"Here, I found it." He tossed me the photo box from my bedside table, me catching it and sliding it in my bag alongside my photo.

"So, you promise you're going to stop talking to him? He caught my arm on my way out of my bedroom.

"Theo!" I scoffed, "I told you. We're working on our relationship; I won't be talking to Miles." I shook my head, worming my way out of his grasp, "I'll see you tonight, okay?" I gave him a quick hug before leaving the house.

"I really don't know where my head is at." I held my head in my hands, after Dr. Taylor asked me the very first question of the session.

"Let's talk about your progress within each of your relationships. Let's start with Theo." She directed at the photo box laid out of the table right in front of us, "Pick it up, and see what feeling it brings you."

I held the box in my hand, feeling a wave of emotion run over me. Nostalgia, happiness, mixed with an element of fear, worry.

"With Theo, I feel so much love and just bliss when I think about our past together, and worry when it comes to the future. We fight so much because of other people in our lives and it's come between us and I'm scared it'll continue to. I have so much love for him and I would do anything for him but-"

"But you don't love him in the way that he wants you to." She finishes my sentence.

"Exactly." I nodded, reflecting on Theo and I's conversation at his parent's beach house, "We had a talk about it but I just don't think he gets it." I shrugged.

"Ellie, as long as you've communicated that with him, and as long as you've done your part there is nothing else you can do to heal the situation." She smiled, then pointed towards the next object on the table.

I placed the photo box down, picking up Miles' hoodie, his smell still lingering faintly on it. I immediately felt a wash of safety wave over me, comfort, a feeling that I only feel around Miles. That safety then lingered into regret. My actions and thoughts so blind by focusing on Theo and our relationship than how Miles could potentially feel about it.

"Miles has helped me with so much, with what I initially came here for. My visions, my family and just anything I had going on I knew I could come to him, and vice versa. I help him with his daughter and he helps me with everything. I just can't- I won't forgive myself if I never get back on track with Theo because of him. It eats away at me."

"With situations where relationships are on the line because of other close relationships, you have to come out of yourself and picture it from an alternative perspective. Seeing yourself with both individuals, seeing the portrayal of your emotions as well as actually *feeling* them. There's no use trying to make yourself happier with someone when there's somebody else you clearly gravitate towards." She spoke, briefly making notes in between sentences.

"And finally..." she continued, pointing towards the photo frame still perched on the coffee table.

I picked it up, my hands shaking slightly, "My dad." My voice croaked.

It honestly feels like a fever dream that I even saw him again, and *everything* that he told me after that.

My breath hitched in my throat, my heartbeat speeding up, double the speed in less than a minute.

"No. Never mind."

# Chapter Thirty-Four

## ELLIE

"Thank God you're alright." He exhaled as if he was holding his breath, waiting for me to answer.

"Do you need me to come in for work?" I bluntly replied, reluctantly keeping my promise to Theo.

"What?" was his only word, defeated and obviously disappointed.

"Brady, do you need something?" I coughed out, my voice almost refusing to speak.

"No. No, I-I was checking in on you. I've- missed you." I could practically envision him choking up, doing the thing the way he blinks away his tears before they even get a chance to fall.

"If you need me for work, you know where to find me, okay?" I took a deep breath with my every word. The bile churned in my stomach at the thought of hurting him.

The angel and the devil on my shoulders were working hard at fighting each other, yelling at me, conflicting and blinding me to the true right decision.

"Can you babysit Maeve tonight?" He spoke up, his voice immediately clearer and colder.

"I have plans tonight, sorry." The emotion wavering through my voice, clearly hitting me more than him now.

It's best to push him away. It's best to push him away. If I want my relationship with Theo to be completely okay, it's best to push him away.

"Right. Right, okay." He hung up instantly without so much of a 'goodbye'. Not that I expected one.

I stared at my phone, zoned out for a minute or so before calling Carly, asking her and Lucas to come over. I needed reassurance that I was doing *something* right. She'll give me the cold hard truth and that's how I'll know what to do.


"I've really done it this time, haven't I?" Tears waterfalled out of my eyes, uncontrollably, no form of power left in me to stop them, "I know you've told me already, Carls, but I just... I feel like I *have* to choose Theo. I've known him for 20 years and- and I've known Miles for, what, 5? I've only liked him for what, two, three months?"

Carly sighed, sitting back on the sofa and rolling her eyes, committing to her act of silence. I get that she's frustrated, God, I would be too if I gave someone advice over and over again just for them to come to me crying when they choose the wrong thing. The wrong thing. It's subconscious, of course I know I'm not choosing the right path. I'm choosing loyalty over happiness. In this situation is that what I need?

Lucas sits down on the other side of me, putting an arm around me, "If you think Theo is what is good for you right now, then go with it, Ellie. Try not to think too hard about it. Don't think about what-ifs. You, more than anyone, deserve to be happy and if he is who makes your little world spin, then let

yourself have it. Let yourself have something good for once."
He rocked us both side to side, running his hand up and down
my arm.

*"Let yourself have me."*

"Since when did you get so wise?" Carly joked, erupting a
laugh from all of us, "For real though, he's right, *bebita.*"

Just as I was about to spring a grateful reply, the door shuffled open, Theo speeding in and briefly stopping beside us,
"Hey, I'm not stopping for long, I'm meeting Olivia for a
coffee. Hope that's okay. Hi, Carly and- I never caught your
name, mate."

"Lucas." He cleared his throat.

It was like my entire life flashed before my eyes when I saw
him, my entire decision making of wrong or right, inevitably
ending on the 'wrong' choice. The realisation hitting me that
I'll never be enough for Theo, nor is there a point in trying to
be. That I should choose my own happiness and what makes
me happy instead of trying to force myself to feel at least a ray of
joy with the wrong person.

"I'm going out too. See you later." I mumbled back to him
as he left the house just as quickly.

Carly squeezed me into a tight hug, giddy and bouncing
for joy, dragging me up, "We'll drive you there ourselves.
Let's go."

Cold, drenched and shivering. In nervousness? Just
because I was cold? In anticipation? All worth it for
what I was about to open the door to. If he would
still accept me. Apologise profusely, beg for his forgiveness and
explain how wrong you were, how blinded you were. The steps

I repeated in my head until the process was disrupted by the front door swinging open.

My mouth opened to begin my practised, processed routine, only to be stunned by the woman standing opposite me.

I stuttered over my words, trying to form some sort of reason why I was here before she spoke first, "Oh, what a doll. You must be Ellie, come in! Come in." Her sweet voice ushered me in, out of the pouring rain, running and grabbing a blanket and wrapping it around me.

"I'm sorry, forgive my excitement. I'm Miles' mum, Anna. I'm staying with him this week. May I just say, you are even more beautiful than he described." She fawned, brushing my drenched hair out of my face.

My jaw remained slightly open, my eyebrows permanently raised, completely shocked at the sudden, unexpected encounter.

"Who is it?" Miles came out of his room, ruffling a towel through his half-wet hair, dressed in a tight t-shirt and baggy joggers.

He pauses in his tracks, visibly swallowing, losing his breath.

Anna glanced between us both, both of us unable to take our eyes off of one another, as if it had been decades since our last meeting.

"I'm going to pop to the shops. I'll be right back, honey." She nods, putting on her jacket and promptly leaving.

He stood still remaining in silence, a look of hurt wavering over him.

"I'm sorry." I manage to spit out, tears already brewing in my eyes, "I thought that if I chose Theo he'd stick to his promises and he'd be good and supportive just like he said. Just like you are. And-And then I realised he'll never change and you've made me feel a way that nobody else ever has even tried to make me feel." I took a breath, noticing my rambling.

His eyebrows pinched, hurt, merging with confusion. Merging with sadness.

"I get if you never want to see me again, I know I was a complete idiot for pushing you away when all you've tried to do is help me over and over again. I get it if you don't want to help me anymore and you want nothing to do with me or," I took a breath, "Okay. Okay, this was stupid I should go, I'm sorry." I dropped the blanket over the coat rack, beginning to leave.

I got out of the door, letting the rain hit me again. Hitting me in every direction, the aggressive surge of wind lashing against me.

I paused, trying to locate Carly's car which she promised to stay until I was ready to go. I paused, waiting for something, some sort of sign which told me I was doing the right thing by coming here. Something telling me to turn around, crawl back to him and give him a chance to see me and be angry. A chance to not want to talk but just be in each other's company.

Before I realised that he did chase after me.

He chased after me, grabbing my wrist and spinning me around. His hair was stuck to his forehead, even more dishevelled than normal. He looked beautiful, even through the chaos and insanity I put him through. No matter how many times I push him away or try to detach myself, he always comes back. He always manages to make me weak at the knees at a single look.

"Please. Don't leave. Not again." I couldn't distinguish from what tears were flowing out of his eyes through the torrential rain thundering around us.

"Miles..." My tears joined his, not even giving me a sign to react or prepare.

I hate the fact that I've made him cry. I hate myself for

giving any sort of negativity or sadness to this man who's done nothing but help me, "You know this isn't helping. You know deep down you can't help me, no matter how hard we try."

He pushed my hair out of my face, firmly grasping my head in his hands, even throughout the brash cold, still bringing warmth to my cheeks.

"All I ever want to do is help you. I exist to help you, please just stay and let me help you."

"I know how much he means to you. And I know choosing me means losing him. But this... this is straight out of a movie, a novel; I don't think either of us would've gotten here without each other. I don't want this to end. Please."

I closed my eyes, embracing myself in his warm touch, allowing myself to fully feel this.

# Chapter Thirty-Five

## ELLIE

"You know, I've not seen him this smiley in a long time." She sat down, placing a mug of tea in front of me, and taking a sip of her own.

I sat up, turning to face her, smiling and taking a sip of my drink, not really knowing how to respond to that.

I quickly was pulled back onto my stomach, laying on the floor as Maeve tugged my shirt, urging me to finish my drawing.

"Oh, while he's not with us, I was thinking of coming back for his birthday, maybe as a surprise party? With a few of your mutual friends from work?"

*Mutual friends?* The man is absolutely feared at work; the only possible solutions for that would probably be Carly and Lucas.

"Yeah, sounds good." I smiled.

"Do you like my drawing?" Maeve whispered, pushing her piece of paper towards me. It was a rough sketch of what I was assuming was me and Miles, who was holding lots and lots of flowers and a scarily wide grin on both of our faces.

"It's beautiful Maeve, you have a talent." I giggled, ruffling her hair and kissing her on the forehead.

The door down the corridor sprung open, dividing all of our attention towards Miles, who was now powering towards us.

"Mum, can you...?" He cocked his head towards Maeve's room, Anna silently nodding, picking up Maeve and her drawing supplies and skipping off to her room.

"Are you okay?" I slowly stood up, becoming more concerned by the second.

"Look at this." He handed me an arrest report.

"Oh my God." I took a minute to read all the information, taking everything in, the unsettling feeling shivering down me, "Oh my God."

The picture in the top left-hand corner immediately surged an eerie aura, nothing completely unfamiliar to me, but something quite troubling instead.

I moved on to the details, confirming exactly what the paranoia and fear in me was screaming at me for me to notice.

*Macy Moore. 27 years old. Arrested on suspicion of multiple murders throughout the below timeframes – cases listed below.*

My feet immediately started pacing around his living room. My heart beat matching every quick step, every quick breath I took, matching the speed in which my brain was running. Trying to figure this out never got better, it never solved itself or got any less complicated, never made me feel less crazy or sociopathic or psychotic, just utterly worse in every way.

"Ellie, you're in your head. Breathe." His voice was almost a whisper to me, a voice pushed out, silenced by the scream of the voice in my head. The tinnitus overpowering him, her, it and everything that anchored me to my reality, the waves crashing against my brain telling me everything I definitely shouldn't be doing. Her voice getting stronger and stronger and-

"Ellie." His hand grabbed my arm, forcing my feet to come to a halt, "Come back to me. Breathe."

We sat down together, his hand running up and down my back, the feeling immediately soothing me.

"She wants to see you." he spoke up after a moment of panicked silence.

"Of course she does." I shook my head, in slight disbelief even though my dad fully prepared me for this moment.

"She- uh- she said, she's never forgotten you, 'like you did to her,'" he quoted, handing me another sheet of paper with an interview transcript written down, "Carly sent me the recording of the interview. She's not willing to say anything until she speaks to you." He sighed, his thumbs twiddling.

"Okay. Okay." I breathed, trying to spiral into a freak out again, "Wait, Carly sent it to you?" His words finally resonated in my brain.

He cleared his throat, breaking eye contact with me and standing up, "Yeah. Uh- yeah."

"Not Prescott? Why isn't he keeping you in the loop?" I asked, standing up to follow him.

He paused, his back still facing towards me, "He's put me on indefinite leave." He sighed, his head bowing.

"What? Why?" I paced round to the front of him, forcing him to face me and make eye contact with me.

"He found out that I was helping you, and well, he said everything is over, I can't come back until, well, I can't go back." He sighed, still avoiding direct eye contact.

"Until what, Miles?" I pushed him, grabbing his hands

"Until I cut you off. Completely. And that's not going to happen, so I'd rather never go back." He finally met my eyes, a look of anger shooting through his expression.

"What?! No. No, no, no. I'm so sorry, you can't, you have

to go back." My breath hitched in my throat, a painful tear pricking my eyes.

The entire time I was out fixing my relationship with Theo, ignoring Miles, he was losing his job. He was upset enough with my stupid way of reacting to wanting my friendship back, with me cutting him off completely, and finding out he's lost his job because of that stupid reason?

"No. It was *my* choice to help you. I stand by that. I don't regret a thing." He grabbed my shoulders, running his fingers in circles, touching our foreheads together.

I sighed, not knowing how to approach this. If I wasn't so focused on going to talk to my murderous cousin, I would be a lot more insistent on having that conversation right here, right now.

"Okay. Prescott would be the most stupid guy alive if he didn't let you talk to her. Your way in is easy. It's what you have to say, that's hard."

# Chapter Thirty-Six

## ELLIE

"It's bad. I know." I sighed, my heart palpitating at a million miles a second.

"Just, be careful, okay? And call me back the second you get out." Theo insisted.

"Promise, I've gotta go." I panned over to Miles, Carly and Lucas stood by the door, glancing over to me.

I made a quick run over to them, taking a deep breath as I stopped next to Carly.

"You've got this." She smiled, rubbing and linking my arm.

Miles and Lucas nodded in sync, a weak, nervous smile showing from them both.

"What if Prescott thinks I'm an accessory?" My thoughts immediately flowed out of my mouth. My mouth running dry, my heart beating into my throat, the panic overriding my last sane thoughts.

"He can't arrest you. He doesn't have enough grounds. I'll be right there; you don't have to worry." She nodded at me, sighing, becoming visibly tense herself.

The door swung open, Prescott standing in the doorway

with a cold glare shared between all of us, "Montana, Parker... Easton. Ready? Brady." He gave Miles a disapproving look, gesturing for the three of us to walk past him.

I shot Miles a final wistful look before Prescott covered my vision of him, smiling condescendingly.

Carly and Lucas paused behind the double doors that Prescott shoved me into, "Remember, I'm always listening." He gritted into my ear, pushing me towards the door. The door in which stood behind the reason behind my worst nightmare for the past 4 months. The reason why my entire world has crumbled and changed for the worst.

I inhaled, holding my breath for as long as humanly possible without becoming even more light-headed than I thought possible. I exhaled, placing my hand on the door handle, slowly making my way inside. I didn't allow myself to properly focus on the face until I took the seat anticipating my arrival in front of her.

My hand settled into one another, placing my hands on the table, mere inches away from my enemy. I swallowed, finally gaining the courage to submerge the bile rising in my throat and look up at her. Make eye contact with her.

Her eyes stared right back into mine, almost like an exact mirror of my own except the expression was sinister, amused, aggravating. It's as if my past suddenly was whiplashed into me the second, I laid eyes on her. The sight of her only heightened my already high senses by one hundred. Drying all the words from my throat, shutting off my brain from all the words I had prepared to speak, restricting all my stable thoughts.

"I see you all the time, Ellie." Her words sent a jolt of shock-horror into me.

"You...see me?" I managed to stumble out.

"Don't pretend like you don't see me too. I see you. I feel you, everywhere. Every time. You watch me." She smiled sadistically, grinning, "How impressed are you with my work, on a scale of 1-10?" She tapped her handcuffed hands on the table expectantly.

"Your...work?" My words wouldn't properly form still, my brain still not consciously registering this situation.

"The *murders.* Apparently that word is a bit taboo here." She giggled.

*And I thought I was insane.*

I remember all the times a figure appeared in my mind, in my visions, the person standing in a hood, the footsteps in the darkness. It was all her.

My mouth hung slightly open, my eyes scanning over her, deeply trying to understand her motive.

"Cat got your tongue?" Her expression quickly turned from a cynical, amused one to a bored, threatening one.

"You've killed all these people, and all you can think about...is me?" I felt sick to my stomach, a sudden sadness overwhelming me. I need to get out of here, and quickly.

"Don't tell me you don't feel it too, you should join me." She smiled sadistically, leaning as close as she could towards me.

"Prescott." I said, looking towards the one-way mirror as a signal to let me out.

No response.

"Prescott?" I called again, a nerve chilling through me, "What did you do?" I turned to face her again, tears filling my eyes.

I scooted my chair back, speeding towards the door and trying to pry it open from this side, but of course, it's impossible.

"You want him gone as much as I did. I only wanted to talk to you for a while." She tilted her head, plastering a fake frown on her face.

I yanked on the door handle, desperate to get a touch of the air outside the suffocation of this room.

"We're both crazy. At least I can admit it. We're Moore's, tell me you don't feel our link." I could hear her voice creeping inside my head, feeling her getting closer behind me by the second, even though it was quite literally impossible.

I spun around, still seeing her sat in the spot at the table with a snarky smile on her face.

"No." was all I managed to say.

"You can't run from me, we're family." She stared into my eyes, gliding right into my soul.

"I'm *not* your family." Tears choked my words. I banged on the door, trying to reach Carly or Lucas' attention.

The door flew open, Carly barged in, flustered, a confused, angry look planted on her face, "He was meant to stay in here with you." She rolled her eyes, turning her back and glancing at the panel, "He didn't press record, he didn't watch you. Where is he?" She looked around, "Please tell me she didn't admit to anything." Carly finally looked at me, realising the colour draining from my cheeks, the life leaving my eyes, "Shit, are you okay?" She brought me into a tight hug, kicking the door shut behind me.

"Now what? She admitted everything. She won't do it again, and I can't talk to her again. Please don't make me go through that again." The waterfalls overfell my eyes, unstoppably, inconsolably.

Carly stood speechless, visibly concerned, "I don't know...I don't know." She ran her hands through her hair.

Miles and Lucas ran in, both looking as concerned as the other. Miles immediately ran over to me, pulling me into his chest and placing a prolonged kiss on my forehead. I could feel his heartbeat against mine, his surprisingly racing twice the speed.

"We can only hold her for 48 more hours." Carly nodded, "Brady, we need you back. I can't do this on my own." Carly pleaded.

Prescott hobbled towards us, grabbing the wall on his way, panting, "I'm sorry, I don't know what happened."

"Brady's taking over. That's what happened." Carly spat at him, rolling her eyes and turning her back on him, forcing Lucas to turn away too.

"Ellie." Miles held my cheeks, "I can come in with you this time. Please, we need this." His eyes glimmered with worry, pain, fear, hope. All mixed into one pleading look.

"Fine. Fine, but you have to be there. Promise you'll be there." I clung onto his hand, the only solid thing keeping me from losing my entire mind.

"I promise. Tomorrow." He looked towards Carly and Lucas, "Tomorrow."

"Changed your mind?" She bit her lip, bouncing in her seat, excitement radiating off of her, "I knew you'd come around, it's in your blood." She grinned.

I looked towards Miles for help, who was standing in the corner of the room behind her, who immediately gave me the perfect reassuring look.

"You've caught me. I'm done watching from afar, Macy, I want to know what goes on in that head of yours. Of...ours." I plastered as comforting of a smile as I could, reaching out and grabbing her hand. The sensation single-handedly made me feel sick. Miles flinched at the contact, taking a few steps towards us, causing Macy to retract from my grasp.

"Your boyfriend doesn't like this very much." She leaned in, whispering and smirking over her shoulder.

"Doesn't matter what he likes. It's our mind, right? What's next?" I smiled, as convincingly as possible. She was smart. She knew what I was trying to do, I had to be tactile about this.

"Getting arrested is the least of my concerns right now, sweetie. I hope you know that. Things will still happen if I go under. When you walk free, we'll merge, we'll be unstoppable." Her eyes widened, her eyebrows raising as if the thought of me committing whatever murders she wanted aroused her.

"Agent Brady." She sang in a sing-song voice, taunting him, "You should keep an eye on this one from now on. Family contact does *funny* things to the brain." She smirked, chuckling under her breath.

*Right Ellie? We'll be together forever.* I felt her voice echo into my head, her lips not moving one bit. I shot back, immediately getting up, feeling bile churning in my stomach, the real proof simply stood in front of me, inside of me, in my head.

She had a sadistic smile plastered permanently on her face, like she knew what was to come. As if she could read my own future better than I could ever even imagine it.

# Chapter Thirty-Seven

## ELLIE

"We've not seen each other in quite a while, how've you been Ellie?" Dr. Taylor smiled.

"It has been a while hasn't it, sorry I've been busy, but it's been good. I've been good." I nodded.

"I'm glad to hear that. How is everything coming along? The visions?" She pulled out her notebook, settling down.

"It's been just over a month since my last one. I feel great actually." I smiled to myself, noting my final peace within myself.

Since Macy was arrested, Miles got his job back, I haven't been having visions and everything has just been perfect. Too perfect, which is why I'm back here. The paranoia was weighing way too heavily on top of me for me to finally be able to enjoy my freedom from the shackles of my visions. As much as it's all over, I feel like I can still hear her voice in the back of my mind. I hear her echo, her whisper in the depth of my ear, simply just an itch that can't be scratched.

"Are you sure? You sort of zoned out on me there." Dr.

Taylor scooted her chair towards me, leaning forwards and tilting her head to the side.

"Yeah, I just, I feel like it's not over? Which is why I've come back. I had to see you again, I don't know."

"Sometimes when you go through traumatic events, the effect of it can linger on for a long time even after the event itself is over. If this is the case, this is completely normal for you, Ellie. Consider it a healing stage, or a recovery stage, it's not necessarily going to be linear, but you'll have off days and then days where you feel on top of the world, and that's completely normal." She shrugged, sinking back into her chair.

"So, I'll be fine?" A wave of relief washed over me.

"For now, yes. You don't know what will happen along the line but we can only hope for the best." She smiled, nodding.

"Here, open wide." Miles dangled a strand of spaghetti in front of me, "Tasty?" He smiled proudly.

"Delicious." I smiled back, enjoying our little domestic moment together.

We had the record playing *My Girl,* our self-proclaimed song, dancing around the kitchen like we had nothing else to do, swaying together, eating our pasta ingredients before we were meant to, this is how life is meant to be. Dancing in the kitchen, pasta and wine nights, with a man I really, *really* like. It's heaven.

"So," I popped a tomato into my mouth, "Your birthday is coming up." I smiled, nudging his shoulder.

"It is." He nodded, avoiding eye contact with me.

"You should have a party, with a few people from work?" I swallowed, deciphering his reaction, "Carly and Lucas maybe?"

He cleared his throat, "Well, Lucas is a great lad, and Carly is your best friend, I'd love it if they came. Maybe Joan and Mark too." He nodded, turning to face me and looking down on me.

"Joan and Mark? Who are they?" I took a step back, trying to remember the unfamiliar names.

"You don't know Joan and Mark?" He chuckled, throwing his head back.

"No, I don't know Joan and Mark, or else I wouldn't have asked who Joan and Mark are if I knew who Joan and Mark were." I emphasised their names, the words starting to sound fake.

"Joan and Mark are starting to sound fake the more we say it." He laughed, reading my thoughts.

"Are you sure Joan and Mark are real?" I taunted him, gasping and pushing at his shoulder.

"Of course Joan and Mark are real. I have friends, you know." He shook his head at me, enveloping me in his arms.

"Gosh, shocker." I gasper dramatically, letting myself warm in his embrace.

We laughed, enjoying each other's grasp for a minute before he pulled away and spun me to face him.

"Are you okay though? I feel like we haven't had a proper conversation since, well since everything." He ran his hand through his hair and then over my head, "It's over, you're okay. You know that, right?"

"Yeah, thank you. It's helped, being here with you. I'm just scared to go back to being alone." I reflect on the time I've spent every waking moment at his house since everything went down, getting into the routine of taking Maeve to school, drawing with her when she gets back, making dinner with Miles and watching a movie. Putting Maeve to bed and staying up talking because we never run out of things to say to each other. Making a mental note that I would have to go home eventually and simultaneously dreading that day.

"You can stay as long as you want. You're forever welcome here." He placed a gentle, prolonged kiss on my forehead, smiling into it.

"I know. But I need to get over this. I'll go home." I took a deep breath, grounding myself.

"And you'll come back?" He inhaled.

"And I'll come back." I nodded into his chest, willingly accepting his embrace.

"You want a drink?" He stood, hovering in his kitchen as I sat on the edge of the sofa, waiting for him to come over.

I felt the awkwardness, or rather nervousness radiating off of him, and it was making me double as anxious.

"Why are you hovering? Just come and sit." I laid back on the sofa, trying to make myself comfortable.

"I just-" He cleared his throat, perching next to me on the sofa, "I know we're over everything that happened, I just feel like I need to have one final *closure* conversation with you." He nodded, as if he was trying to convince himself this was the right direction to go.

"Oh. Okay." I nodded slowly, sighing, not expecting that this was what he called me for.

"I'm just going to talk, and you're going to listen. Okay?" He grabbed both my hands, nodding frantically.

"Okay." I matched his nodding pace, a nervous smile breaking out.

"So, obviously, seeing Olivia a few months ago stirred up some old feelings between us, and I am so aware of how wrongly I went about that, especially when we were together, so I'm sorry about that." He took a quaky breath, "I really like her, and I really want to pursue something with her, and as my best friend, and the person who means the most to me in this entire world, I wanted your approval. Especially after everything." He exhaled like it was his last breath.

In sync with him, I exhaled, holding my breath as if he was about to tell me my non-existent dog died.

I stayed silent for a second, properly digesting what he said, a smile taunting my lips, "Theo." I started, "I want you to be happy. That's the only thing, if Olivia makes you happy, then that's exactly what I want for you." I pulled him into a tight hug, tears pricking my eyes as I heard his gigantic exhale.

"We could've avoided all this if I wasn't so annoying and jealous. I'm sorry." He chuckled, borderline crying, "And Miles. He's good for you?"

"He's so good for me." A blush rose on my cheeks.

"I'm sorry I couldn't be what you needed, but I'm so happy that he is." He held my head in his hands.

"You've been absolutely everything to me for the past 20 years, I think it's okay if we have other people." I chuckled through pooling tears, "I feel like we've both been scared because I don't know about you, but I would rather die than lose you completely, and I think that blinded us both into forcing ourselves into something we, deep down, knew wasn't meant to be." I confessed, refusing to make eye contact with him until the last word.

He paused, "I guess I let my love *for* you confuse being in love with you. I always want the best for you no matter how I show it." He brought our foreheads together, "I do love you, Ellie. Don't know where I'd be without you." He mumbled.

"Love you too, Theo."

# Chapter Thirty-Eight

## ELLIE

"Happy Birthday sweetheart!" Miles' mum burst through the door, almost giving him a heart attack.

"Mum! You're back!" He regained his breath, chuckling and bringing her into a hug.

She gestured for me to come over, looking over Miles' shoulder with a beaming grin on her face, "Ellie it's so lovely to see you again, honestly, dear, you're glowing." She pulled me into her and Miles, snuggling against us, before she spotted Maeve across the room, gasping in awe and going over to her and Betty.

A loud bang startled me, Carly waving a bottle of Prosecco in the air with Lucas grinning next to her.

"Ellie! How've you been? We've missed you!" Joan screeched in my direction coming over to me with Mark glued to her side.

I plastered a smile on my face, pretending that I actually knew who they were, going over to greet them whilst hearing a chuckle stem from Miles behind me.

The evening was filled with laughter and drinks, bubbles

specifically, dancing and horrible karaoke. I sat on the sofa, watching Lucas and Carly sing *Lay all your love on me* by ABBA to each other, a bit too passionately, and definitely drunkenly as Maeve came bouncing over to me whispering, "It's time, it's time, it's time." With an excited grin on her face.

I grabbed Carly, pulling her to the side as she handed her karaoke microphone to Maeve on her way down from our makeshift stage in front of the fireplace.

"Excuse mee! Daddy and Daddy's friends! Pay attention!" She shouted into the mic, not quite getting the concept that her voice would be louder without her shouting.

As she wished, all the attention in the room landed on her, a few curious whispers scattered around the room.

"Okay, ready?" She looked over to Carly and I standing by the speaker.

We nodded, hitting play and starting to act out the choreography we went through with her over the course of the past week or so.

She started doing her grand movements, swinging her arms and legs about while belting Let It Go from Frozen, with Carly mimicking her every movement.

Lucas strolled over, whispering to both of us, "Kinda hard choreography for a, like, 5-year-old, no?" he laughed at Carly's utter and unbreakable focus.

"She's 7." I corrected him.

"She's fine." Carly added on.

I looked over to Miles, a clear, proud yet amused smile on his face as he nodded along to the beat.

Maeve ended with a spin and jazz hands, triggering an eruption of applause and cheers from our little audience, her immediately running into her dad's arms, giggling.

I walked over to the two of them, giving Maeve a rub on the

back and a huge squeeze, "That was amazing, just like we practised." I smiled.

"I know. It was perfect, wasn't it." She bounced in Miles' arms, leaning backwards onto me.

She wriggled out of his arms, skipping over to Carly and dancing round in a circle with her and Lucas.

"They'd be great parents." Miles said into my ear, both of us admiring how soft they were being with Maeve, "Do you ever want children?" Miles cleared his throat, turning to face me.

"I've not really ever thought about it." I lied, immediately trying to change the subject. I had thought about it, and I never wanted to, out of pure fear that I would end up being as bad of a mother as mine was. The fear and sheer paranoia neglected the thought, until I met Maeve. It felt so natural to care and to look after her and just love her.

Lucas stumbled over to us, almost crashing into me and grabbing my shoulder for some sort of stability, "Look at her. She has the prettiest smile." He fawned over Carly who was also on her way over to us, "You have the prettiest smile actually. Doesn't she have the most gorgeousest smile?" he slurred towards Miles.

"Flattery will get you nowhere, mi amor, but grammar... and maybe soberness, will." She laughed, slinking his arm over her shoulder, "I'm going to take him home, happy birthday again, Brady." She smiled, trying to hold up Lucas' weight with her one arm.

Joan and Mark, admittedly who I forgot were there, made their way out shortly after Carly and Lucas, leaving Maeve crashed, fast asleep on the sofa and Betty and Anna cleaning up in the kitchen.

I instinctively stepped over to Maeve, gently picking her up with the blanket wrapped around her, walking down the hall to her bedroom and tucking her in.

I felt Miles' eyes on me as I ruffled her hair, moving back towards the door and shutting it behind me, suddenly finding myself a lot closer to Miles than I thought I would be.

"Thank you." He muttered, almost silent.

"For what?" I whispered back, our proximity making me feel like we had to be quiet.

"I'm- I'm not sure, everything? The whole day. You've made it perfect. I don't think Maeve's ever been that knocked out." He chuckled under his breath.

"Yeah, I think Carly and I went slightly overboard with dance practice." I laughed, recalling all the frantic times we'd practice after school, not knowing how long we had until Miles got home from work.

"So that's what you were doing all those times you were watching her after school?" He snickered, tucking a strand of hair behind my ear.

"Well, that, amongst other things. There were the paintings and the drawings, just endless arts and crafts to be honest and-" I was cut off by the gentlest kiss brought to my lips. A soft yet so passionate and emotional.

"What was that for?" I mumbled through a smile, keeping our closeness but removing our lips from one another.

"You just..." he stumbled over his words for a second, looking for the right thing to say, "You manage to make everything so effortless, Ellie. The way you care about Maeve and the way that you care about me...it's like you were made to fit in with us." A smile crept onto his face.

"Miles, that's so, you're so sweet. I-I don't know what to say."

"I think." He swallowed, taking a deep breath, "I think I'm

falling in love with you. No, No I take that back. Actually, Ellie, I'm so hopelessly in love with you."

My face flushed, immediately making me hot, a chill surging through my body. The words I wasn't expecting to hear but are the only right words for this moment. Nothing fits more than this, than us. Like a piece of a puzzle, like a key to a lock or a ring to a finger. A perfect fit.

"I love you." He repeated, as if he wanted to get it off his tongue a million times over.

"I love you too." The words instinctively rolled off my tongue, as familiar as nothing had ever felt familiar before.

A silence settled over us both, simply admiring one another and a faint pattering distracted us both from outside.

"Can you hear that?" I whispered trying to keep the peace.

Anna suddenly jumped into our sight, "It's snowing outside!" A gleam spread across her face.

The music still echoed from the living room, springing a smile onto Miles' face, "Dance with me?" He held out his hand for me to hold.

"Okay." I shook my head, taking his hand, suddenly realising how movie or book-esque my life has become since seeing Miles. It's just so perfect. My brain is screaming at me that it's too perfect, but there is absolutely nothing that could destroy us, this, ever. If I have a say in how this relationship keeps going, if I can control it, nothing will get in our way.

He pulled me out the front door, the snow already settling on the ground, running hand in hand like two lovestruck teens chasing endless sunsets. Chasing anything but simplicity, chasing anything but silences. The silence that embodied the life which the visions brought alongside them, the crippling loneliness which ate away at me, no matter who I surrounded myself with. Gone. With his hand in mine, I'll never feel silence again. To say the least, my brain is at rest.

*"Baby, it's cold outside."* Miles hummed along to the Christmas songs playing on the radio inside, swaying us side to side.

His voice snapped me out of my thoughts, reminding me of the chilling cold, and the harsh waves crashing onto the shore behind us.

The waves. Crashing and thrashing against the rocks, getting tougher by the minute.

I spun my head round, allowing myself to fly out of Miles' grasp and completely turn my back to him.

I stepped closer, noticing a darkness shadowing a circle of the sea, floating in the midst of an eerie silence. I crouched down, suddenly finding myself at the edge of the shore, the waves running over my feet threatening to pull me in alongside the shadow.

"I've lost you, where've you gone?" Miles whispered into my ear.

I suddenly felt his grasp on me again, in the same position as if it had never left. Never changed. Never let go, still swaying along to the radio, making smudged footprints in the snow.

I turned to face behind me, seeing Anna pottering around the house, lighting the fire and holding a mug, the light from the house seeming so warming, comforting and inviting. But no ocean. Not one in sight. Not a wave, or a touch of the shallows and oceanic shadows in sight.

"Sorry, I'm just in my head." I made eye contact with him, trying to ground myself back into this reality.

"Can I take you out of it?" He pressed our foreheads together, sighing.

"Please, do." A smile formed on my lips, his warmth radiating onto me.

"I want you to be mine. Only mine. I want you to stay with me, forever, and fit even further into our little fantasy. Knowing you has been like a dream, and I want to make it my forever reality. Please?" He kept his voice low, the sound of the snow settling almost covering him.

"I am forever, and always have been yours, Miles. Fantasy, dream or reality. I'm yours." My heart surged in my chest, the heat radiating off of us strong enough to melt the snow around us. My chest immediately felt lighter, a weight lifted off my shoulders. A choice which was long awaited and such an obvious choice it was. Forever Miles Brady's.

"I've been meaning to ask you actually." We stopped swaying and pulled away from one another, suddenly realising how cold it actually is.

He pulled me inside, sitting me down in front of the fire and wrapping a blanket around us both, "Where my mum lives, it's by the seaside. I think it'll be really nice for us to get away for a bit. A change of scenery. Just me, you and Maeve. There's a lake that freezes over where we skate and the snow on the beach is just absolutely magical. I think you would love it." He suggested, taking his hand in mine.

The thought of being near the seaside after *whatever* I just experienced outside does indeed send a chill through me, my subconscious telling me to say no. But what excuse do I have? I should've learnt by now not to trust my inner voice so all I can say is, "I'd love to."

# Chapter Thirty-Nine

## ELLIE

Aside from the endless Disney song marathons from Maeve, the conversational part of the journey was close to nothing. It's as if Miles could tell there's something wrong, his hand squeezing mine the entire journey, reassuring glances exchanged every few minutes with a touching smile.

My heart was in my throat the entire journey, pounding and suffocating any remaining air which could've easily passed through to calm me.

"Excited?" Miles whispered, the silence of the car breaking after Maeve finally crashed from her performances.

"Mhm!" I forced a smile back, my leg bouncing underneath his grasp.

His eyes broke from the road for a second, shooting me a concerned glance, his eyes flickering from my face to my leg subconsciously shaking then back to the road.

I managed to force a breath into me, regaining control over my body, allowing myself to settle my restlessness, "Sorry. I am excited, just a bit...paranoid. It feels weird being... I don't know, free?" I sighed, glancing out of the window, seeing the ocean come into view.

Suddenly I was right back where I left off, the cold water running over my toes, the dark shadow looming, hovering, in front of me. The waves rippling, creating white drifts of foam, covering every inch of the blue deep there once was surrounding me.

I saw bubbles pop up to the surface, the waves suddenly getting progressively more aggressive, threatening to pull me in alongside each pulling current.

"Okay?" Miles finished his sentence, my brain only focusing on that final word.

It's not over and I know it. There is still a part of my mind tearing me away from my sanity. My freedom. Just like the rough waves, each trembling thought manages to pull me further and further away from where I am physically. It's not over.

"You're right. This will be great." I faked my response, smiling at him, hoping to all above that it would satisfy a good response, or make sense at all.

He smiled, nodding and exhaling, turning his full attention back onto the road, "We're almost there anyway. We'll go skating, then sit on the beach for a bit. Sounds good?"

"Sounds good." I replied, my eyes focused on the ocean mere metres away from the window.

"I can't skate. I don't know why I didn't mention that before." I wobbled, gripping onto Miles' arms like it was my last breath.

He throatily chuckled, skating backwards whilst pulling me

along, "You'll get used to it. The more we come here, the more you'll learn." He turned, placing my hands on his waist, allowing myself to trail behind him without any effort whatsoever.

Maeve skated next to us, showing off her spins and arabesques to me, making me wobble simply at the sight of her tricks.

Within a few minutes, my feet had gone sore, my body had gone achy and I was completely knocked out, and still with 30 more minutes to our 'session'.

"I'm going to sit down." I shouted over Miles' shoulder.

"Okay, want me to come with you?" He paused, skating me over to the side, where there were little benches scattered around the edge of the lake.

"No, it's okay, you two enjoy." I attempted to tiptoe and give him a kiss on the cheek, forgetting about the death-blades strapped to my feet and almost taking both of us down.

He sat me down, absolutely trying not to laugh in my face and rushed off to skate with Maeve. Honestly it was quite impressive, kind of like a hockey style sprint and she's a mini figure skater in the making.

I pulled my phone out, my fingers frosty and slightly shaking and called Theo. He and Olivia are off to New York this weekend and then we all, *yes all,* meaning Miles, Maeve and I, Olivia and Theo and Carly and Lucas are going to spend Christmas together. I'm not sure how much of a great idea this is, but considering Theo and I are going to try and make it work, that's all that should matter.

"Hi, Els! How are you?" He promptly answered the phone, cheerfully.

"Hey, T, I'm good. Just sitting, feeling like my feet are going to fall off, no biggie." I laughed, trying to enunciate my pain.

"Let me guess, you aren't really a heels person, so, ice skating?" He laughed down the line.

"Spot on. Get me out of here." I groaned over exaggeratedly, "How are you?"

"Good. Liv and I are on our way to Times Square, going to do some last-minute Christmas shopping then head to some tree lighting annual festival." He explained.

"Ooh, sounds like fun. Take lots of pictures for me." I smiled, completely genuinely, probably for one of the first times I haven't felt remotely a pang of jealousy towards Olivia. I don't know what that ever was, to be honest. Maybe just some internalised fear of losing Theo? And now we've actually talked it out and communicated everything? We're practically perfect in every way.

"Will do. *Hiii, Ellieee!*" A second voice echoed from the distance of the call.

"Hiii, Oliviaaa," I mimicked her tone, "Have fun today."

"Thanks, Els. I'll call you later. Love you." He said confidently.

"Bye, Theo." I hung up quickly, not knowing how Olivia would feel about the whole girl best friend turned lovers turned just friends saying love you to one another.

"We feel bad that you're just sitting here. Want to head to the beach?" Miles and Maeve stood directly in front of me, scaring all my breath out of me.

"God, you scared me. Okay, sounds good." I grabbed his hand, hobbling over to the shoe stand and re-exchanging our shoes for our own.

" I didn't realise how close your mum's house was to the beach." We stood on the sand, right on her front porch whilst also a few long paces away from the seafront.

"You stay here, I'm just going to put Maeve's skates inside. Maybe make hot chocolate. Want one?" He offered.

I shook my head, admiring the view. He was right. The snow on the beach was mind-blowing. It felt like some kind of movie. Something that's scripted, something that you aren't really meant to see in real life.

Miles and Maeve's presence left my side and retreated into the house.

I felt almost what could be described as nothing less than a gravitational pull towards the ocean. The snow burrowed in a thick line where the waves stopped. I cleared a path, suddenly feeling a presence surrounding me again. A voice, *her* voice entering my head, or my surroundings. I couldn't quite tell the difference, or *feel* the difference.

*Do it.*

My head spun around, feeling a figure looming over me. The same shadow which hovered right by my feet, pulling me into the ocean. A dark, looming aura just waiting for me to slip up, allowing itself back into my brain. It was like she was here all over again, taunting me, pushing me to be like her. Getting into my head more than my own thoughts and consciousness are.

I stood right by the waves, my body not able to hold itself upright, the slightest gust of wind making me fall to my knees.

"Are you okay?"

*Do it.*

Another pull towards the ocean, at first, I felt the cold snow, or water, around my ankles, covering my boots, until that was washed away by the cold-water sensation, brushing back and forth against me.

*Drown it.*

Drowning every last recessed emotion, every last haunting demon in my head, every last voice. Every last murder. I could physically feel his hand on my shoulder, taunting me, pushing me down. I could see her shadow in my peripheral vision, not even wanting to look behind to see her figure. I just wanted her gone.

Every last vision. Gone.

*Kill it.*

Her smooth, tempting voice snaked its way back into my mind, my hands suddenly surging under water, with a pressure to hold down like nothing I've ever felt before. To keep drowning it. To keep pushing it underwater. Keep it underwater and it won't ever resurface, let it float out to the horizon never to be seen again.

They thrashed against me, begging to be released, but only one of us could be freed from this. I had to choose me, this life, my sanity, I had to choose me. I have to let my emotions drown. *I have to let him drown.*

My eyes pricked with tears, the sensation and the salty air surging a sting through them. Today was going to be the end of it all, an entire ocean in front of me and the power was in my hands, the control, not even the waves were able to drown out the silence.

They tried to regain control, but my grasp around its neck was too strong for it to escape. Their thrashing limbs slowly becoming weaker and weaker against me, the numbness, the darkness, the silence within me escaping into them. Their darkness, their silence.

I felt a body go limp underneath my hands, the bobbing of the ocean suddenly sending a chill up my spine. The red anger which covered my sense of reality lifted, allowing me to regain consciousness of my surroundings. It was as if a veil was cleared, my mind had never felt so free, so lifted, so cleansed.

*But I passed it on.*

*It stopped because I passed it on. Just like Henry and Rose. Just like Penelope and Edward.*

A flashback hit me, when I first found out about my family being...well, insane. *Every first-born daughter has killed their partner, or in 'mysterious circumstances' since 1868.* I remember Miles flicking through the documents on the endless Moore family history.

They all passed it on.

I blinked, looking to my frost-ridden hands still grasped on the collar of a man, the waves rushing over us both.

I gasped, almost to a choke, where I couldn't possibly take in any more air. His body lay limp, the only movement was the sea surrounding him, moving him.

I recall the voice in my head, sounding a bit too real and startling me, my mind immediately crossing it out.

I shuffled back, allowing the looming shadow to drift out to sea, with every wave getting closer with every darkness and a silence like never before surrounding me, forcing me to retreat into my head.

After all, she had gotten into my head, just like she said. She had complete and utter control over me, just as she warned me she would. My naivety believed it was all over

*Chapter Forty*

S he sat, knees cradled into her chest, rocking back and forth. The world surrounding her, ever so loud with her world crashing down in the most deafening silence. A shadow, cast out to see, never to be seen by a human's eye again. A shadow that she was responsible for. That she laid her problems into and sent to the sunken city.

Her shakes became physical, the tears streaming down her face as her mouth opened, gaping for any sort of air to reconcile her thoughts.

Her person, her reconciliation, her safety and her solace stepped out, immediately noticing and closing the little girl inside the house. He rushed over to her, without a second of hesitation, spinning her to face him.

She couldn't believe her eyes. It was like an *angel* right before her, heaven-sent to the moment right when she needed him most. She reached out, touching him, hands running from his arms to his face, trying to gain some sort of composure how she normally would when she was around him. Nothing succeeded.

ELOUISE BAXTER

He helped her to stand, her wavering figure falling right through him, barely able to pick herself up and before either of them knew it, she'd re-dropped to her knees, unconsciously sobbing, tears flooding out of her, in silence.

Between all of the silences she'd experienced, this had by far been the worst. A quaking, wrenching silence which she could only beg to scream for help. All the moments and visions, leading up to this one singular break.

A fracture in time, a fracture in this very still moment, to change her future forever. But in this moment, in this silence, all that was fractured was his frantic voice.

"Ellie. Ellie. What's wrong? You need to tell me what's wrong." He scanned her, his voice carried through the wind, thinking she was hurt, thinking she had hurt herself, thinking of all the worst-case scenarios aside from what actually happened.

"Daddy, is she okay?" The young girl stepped out of the house, peering from the front porch, "Ellie, is Daddy okay?"

The ripples of the water allowed the lifeless shadow to form, bobbing to the surface, drifting closer and closer to the horizon, the man joining Ellie in her pale physicality.

"I think I did something bad, Miles." She choked, holding him limp in her arms.

*The End.*

*Acknowledgments*

The process of writing this book has been unimaginable, the highs and lows and the pride I feel for finishing something that I have always wished for since I was a little girl. This book would not have been able to happen without a select few of my closest friends and of course, my family.

Firstly, I would like to thank someone who has constantly reassured me, within myself and within my writing. Who pushed me every day and made me believe that I could achieve my dream. Thank you, Jan, for every word you've ever said and all the endless encouragement you've given me.

I would like to thank my friends, who are also my beta readers, Niamh, Sofia, Maine and Mylla. I couldn't ask for a better support group and people to involve in both my writing process and my life. You all have the ability to always put a smile on my face and make me laugh no matter the occasion. My favourite group chats ever. You inspire me. <3

I'd like to thank Mia, Eve and Zil, my bookstagram friends who have supported me throughout my journey, who are constantly being my hype girls and showering me with love and confidence.

To my ARC team, I couldn't have asked for a better group of individuals to have read my book early, you all have really enhanced my writing experience and provided me with excellent feedback.

To Sienna and Olana, who have had to deal with me always

talking their ears off with new ideas and delusions every single day, right from the get-go, you guys are the best!

To my friends at university, my housemates who have to deal with my aggressive typing, thank you for seeing and believing in who I am.

The most important thank you for me is to my Mum, my Dad and my Sister, Becky who from the moment I could talk have always listened to me (no matter how quietly I spoke), who have always encouraged me to be true to myself and motivated me in any hobbies and skills I wanted to take up, no matter how short-lived they were, whilst also been my number one supporters behind this book and throughout my life.

I would also like to especially thank my Aunty Lissi and Great Aunty Jenny; my Grandmothers Yia-yia, and my Gran-Gran for never letting me fail to see my potential and constantly reminding me that whatever I want to do is achievable 'if I put my mind to it, I can do it'. This book would not have been possible without the support of my ENTIRE family, thank you and I love you all so much.

To my late Grandad and Nanny, I'll always try my best and hardest to live up to be "the greatest" for you. To my late Grandad Tim, for quietly inspiring me to acknowledge and act on my creativity.

Lastly, I would like to thank everyone who has ever taken the time to read this book, I trust that my work, my characters and their lives, is safe in your hands. Thank you to everyone who has followed me, read even a page of my book and supported me. You all mean the world to me and none of this would've been possible without any of you.

Printed in Great Britain
by Amazon

41434048R00148